D1343288

Late Summer Love

Book 3 in The Guesthouse Girls Series

Judy Ann Koglin

Maui Shores Publishing

Kihei 2020

This book is a work of fiction. The characters within are fictitious. Any resemblance to any particular person is purely coincidental.

Summer Entanglements Copyright © 2020 by Maui Shores Publishing

Kihei, HI 96753
http://www.mauishorespublishing.com

Unless otherwise indicated, Scripture quotations are from: *The Holy Bible*, American Standard Version (ASV)

Library of Congress Control Number: 2020922105

ISBN 978-1-953799-04-3 (paperback)
ISBN 978-1-953799-05-0 (e-book)

CHAPTER ONE

Sealing the Deal

"Thank you so much! We had so much fun. We haven't been on a jet ski in years!" the female customer told Hope as she handed her back the damp lime green and black life jackets that she and her husband had used for the last hour. "We'll have to come back again next time we are in Chelan. We come the same week each August. Do you have a business card?"

Hope Stevens handed the lady a glossy white business card printed with "Joe's Jet Skis and Boat Rentals" in red letters. "Here you go! Thanks for coming by!" Hope said to the couple as they headed to their car.

After the customers left the check-out shack, Hope noticed that, hooked securely to one of the life jacket straps, was a set of keys.

1

"Oh, wait!" she called after them. She jogged the 50 yards to the parking lot where the two had almost reached their car, Hope's dark blonde ponytail swaying as she jogged. "Are these yours?"

"Oh yes, thanks!" the man confirmed.

Hope deposited the keys in his outstretched hand. "You're welcome!" She grinned as they went on their way.

While she was in the parking lot area, her Uncle Joe, the owner of the watercraft rental business, pulled up in his Jeep. Hope noticed that he was dressed in a pair of slacks and a polo shirt, a bit nicer than his normal faded shorts and t-shirt.

"Hope," Joe said, "the final meeting for buying the store is today. Since you're a church goer now, how 'bout you talk to the Man upstairs for me? I could use all the help I can get at this meeting!" he joked as he headed across the street for his meeting in the sporting good store's office.

Today, Uncle Joe and his attorney, Anne Walton, were in the final stages of negotiations towards buying the sporting goods store across the street from his boat rental shop. If the deal went through, Hope would get to stay in town permanently, instead of just for the summer, because her mom Megan would move here and help run the sporting goods store with her brother Joe.

Hope knew that Uncle Joe was half-joking about the prayer, but she decided it certainly wouldn't hurt to try. She went into the shack and quietly prayed, "Lord, I don't know if you are listening, but if you are, and you can help Uncle Joe and his lawyer to have a good meeting so that he can buy the store and we can move here, I'd be very grateful. Thanks for letting me come here this summer. Um…amen."

Once she hesitantly finished her prayer, she opened her eyes. As she did, she saw a family arrive for their jet ski session. She scanned the log and prepared their paperwork to be signed.

Over the next few hours, the shop continued to be hopping with tourists arriving for their sessions, and Hope and her coworkers kept things moving efficiently.

Three hours later, Hope looked up and happened to see Uncle Joe and his attorney as they emerged from the meeting and stood on the sidewalk in front of the store. The two of them were chatting intently. Joe had a smile on his face when he caught Hope's eye from across the street, and he held up a red folder to her. Hope wasn't sure about the contents of the folder, but she knew that he looked very happy. That was enough to tell her that he was going to be able to buy the store.

3

She saw him shake hands with Anne and hand the folder over to her as she got into her car and left for her law office in Wenatchee.

It continued to be a busy day, but in between customers, Uncle Joe was able to tell Hope that the deal they struck exceeded his expectations. He said that the sporting goods store's current owners really wanted him to succeed and agreed to work with him and Megan to make sure that they knew everything they needed to know. The current owners were planning to remain in town for the next year in case Joe had questions. They did not need to get all the money from the sale of the store immediately, so they had worked out a good payment plan, and Joe stated that he planned to pay it off early if at all possible. "At five o'clock, your mom will be off work and we can Facetime her and share the good news."

"Then I can tell my friends, right?" Hope begged.

"Yes, the papers have been signed! It's a done deal, and we'll officially transition ownership in October. Your roommate Emma can even interview me for her paper or whatever she wanted to do. Now, she will have a bigger story than just boat rentals."

"It's a blog, Uncle Joe. 'Emma's Business Blog.' She'll be thrilled to write a piece about your new venture," Hope assured him.

Uncle Joe and Hope video called her mom at five that evening.

"Hi Megan," Joe began.

"Is it good news or bad news?" Megan questioned.

"Neither" Joe countered, "It's *great* news! The sellers are really cool and they have agreed to stick around so we can be trained before they move."

"What do you think, Mom? We get to start our new life here in Chelan!" Hope exclaimed with excitement that belied her typically quiet demeanor.

"Well, it's definitely the best news I've heard so far today," Megan agreed happily. Hope and her mom both had happy tears as they celebrated, and Uncle Joe was excited as well. "So, what's our next move?" Megan looked at her brother for direction.

"I suggest that you quit your weekend job now but keep your regular job at the plant in Lynnwood for the time being. When you're available on weekends, you can drive up here to Chelan sometimes to start training in the store with the current owners. They have offered to train you whenever you can come."

"That sounds like a good idea, as long as my car will make it. I don't know how many miles she has left on her," Megan admitted.

"Make sure you have towing insurance and if you need any car repairs, we'll deal with it," Joe promised.

After a few more exchanges, they hung up and Hope headed back to her room at The Guesthouse, and Uncle Joe turned his attention to some walk-in customers.

****

When Hope got home, she couldn't wait to tell her friends her great news.

Aunty Nola, The Guesthouse's owner, was home. She was one of the few people who already knew that the sporting goods store sale was in the works, but now that it was official, she gave a big sigh of relief.

"I am so glad that we get to keep you around!" Aunty Nola gushed. Autumn is a lovely season here. I can't wait for you to experience the apple harvest." She had already offered to let Hope stay with her in The Guesthouse free of charge until November when Hope's mom would move to Chelan, and the two of them could move into the house that Uncle Joe was buying from his landlord.

Aunty Nola wasn't really her aunt, nor anyone else's aunt, but she was a beloved member of the town and had been known by that name for years.

"I'm relieved it worked out, too," Hope agreed, giving Nola a hug. "I can't wait to tell the girls!"

She did not wait long because just then, Kendi and Amie, two of her roommates, arrived. Kendi's long, reddish wavy hair caught the early-evening light and contrasted with Amie's short, blonde bob.

Kendi Arnold, a sixteen-year-old girl from Redmond, was in Chelan to work at Brandon's Coffee and Bakeshop. She was gifted in art and music, and she was intelligent and organized.

Amie Larson was a cheerful local girl, born and raised in Chelan. She was staying at The Guesthouse this summer while her parents were in Montana taking care of her mom's dad, Grandpa Peterson while he recovered from a back injury. Amie's parents rented their large house on Lake Chelan to a family from out of state this summer, and the rent money would be a good contribution to Amie's college fund.

Once the girls greeted each other, Hope asked, "Do you know when Emma's getting home?"

"Yes, she'll be home soon," Amie commented. "She was just finishing up interviewing my aunt and uncle for a story about the history of the resort.

I can't wait to read all her articles when she makes her blog public." Amie washed her hands and stretched her five-foot-long body as high as she could to reach the plates down from the middle shelf so the girls could set the table for dinner.

"I have a big surprise for everyone tonight," Kendi announced. "My mom sent me a couple big packages yesterday, but they're actually for all of us. She went shopping at Bellevue Square and found a store that was going out of business and having a huge clearance sale. She bought tons of cute clothes for really cheap. She sent them to me and said to let all of you choose some of them. I thought it would be fun to take pictures of all of us modeling our new clothes to send my mom, too!"

"Oh my gosh, I can't wait to see all the clothes!" Amie exclaimed, her blue eyes sparkling. "I'm going to need a bigger closet," she laughed.

Just then, they heard the creaking of the front door followed by some quick light footsteps, and then, Emma Martinez, their other roommate, burst into the kitchen. "What's for dinner?" she asked. "I'm starving! Oh, and I brought home some amazing ice cream," she remembered, opening the freezer door and searching for a place to squeeze in the quart-sized container of chocolate ice cream filled with a variety of crushed candy bar mix-ins.

"I worked in the ice cream area today, and Mr. Femley let me make my own creation to bring home. He said to tell you hi."

"Oh, George is so sweet," Aunty Nola chuckled, putting the ice cream into the freezer. "We have a lot of excitement this evening."

"What else is going on?" Emma asked.

The girls quickly brought her up to speed about the clothing boxes Mrs. Arnold had sent them.

"There is another thing that Hope will share at dinner," Aunty Nola announced, "let's sit down and eat. I think it is your turn to say grace, Emma."

Emma Martinez was an enthusiastic girl from Pasco, Washington. She was staying at The Guesthouse this summer while she worked at Femley's General Store.

Emma thanked God for the food and the new clothes. After she said "amen," she quickly demanded, "Now, tell us your news, Hope!"

Hope told the whole story—from her mom telling her way back at their Wenatchee shopping trip to her uncle closing the deal this morning—as the other girls' eyes got bigger with surprise, and then, Hope finished, "So I'm going to be with Aunty Nola a little longer than we expected." She glanced at Aunty Nola who beamed back at her.

The other girls shrieked in excitement and had a million questions. Hope told them everything she knew so far.

"So, where did you say you were going to live?" Emma inquired.

"At my uncle's house on Long Avenue. He had been renting a room from the same lady for many years and apparently the rent he was paying was counting toward paying for the whole house. He just paid it off. His landlady is going to keep living there and paying him rent until she moves down south to live with a relative this fall. When she moves out, he gets the whole house, and I will stay in one bedroom and my mom will get another bedroom and Uncle Joe will stay in the same room where he is now," Hope explained again.

"What about your soccer team?" Kendi asked.

"Since I'm staying here, I'll try out for their team," Hope replied humbly.

Amie was probably the most excited about the news because one of her summer roommates would now be living full-time in her town and going to her high school. "Oh, Hope, I'll introduce you to everyone at Chelan High, and you'll have so many friends. It'll be so great to have you here! I'm sure the coaches will be glad to have a new athlete."

"I'm really excited, it just doesn't seem real," Hope spoke quietly. "My mom is coming this Monday to get me registered for school."

"This is such good news!" Emma said while grabbing bowls and spoons for everyone. "I think it calls for some ice cream!"

After devouring their dessert, everyone declared Emma's chocolate candy bar ice cream "perfect." They cleared the table and quickly put the dishes in the dishwasher so they could tear into the boxes of clothing.

"I haven't even opened these packages yet myself," Kendi revealed. "Let's dig in!"

The girls opened the boxes among *ooos* and *ahhhs*. The girls took turns choosing their favorite clothing items like they were drafting players for a team. Each girl got five items from the shipment of tops, dresses, skirts, and shorts. The girls all wore a size small, even though they each had a different body type. Hope was long and lean with long, dark blonde hair; Kendi was medium height; Amie was short with a tiny bone structure, and Emma was short like Amie, but curvy with long, dark, perfectly curly hair and dark eyes.

Mrs. Arnold had sent some special pieces for Aunty Nola packaged separately, including some slacks, blouses, and a lightweight sweater.

Kendi explained that her mom Beth loved to shop, but she had enough clothing of her own for four people, so her husband Phil suggested that she shop for others instead of herself. Kendi's mom liked the idea because she could satisfy her shopping urge and help others at the same time.

The girls hurried upstairs to prepare for the fashion show. Aunty Nola sat on the sofa, and the girls each took a turn walking down the steps wearing one of her new garments. They had a lot of fun and giggled incessantly. Aunty Nola took group pictures of the girls in each round of the fashion show. The girls took photos of Aunty Nola with her outfits, and Amie remarked that she hoped she looked as fit as Aunty Nola did when *she* was 70. They texted the images to Mrs. Arnold with enthusiastic thank yous for her generosity.

As the girls were going up to bed, Kendi asked Hope, "Do you think you will be homesick for your life and your friends back in Lynnwood?"

"I've thought about that. There are a few girls from the soccer team who are really nice that I will miss playing with, but overall, I don't have too many real friends–at least, not until I came here this summer," she said with a grin of realization. She then suggested, "Hopefully, both you and Emma can come visit us here in Chelan sometime.

Maybe we can even go snowboarding! I've never done that, but now that my uncle is going to own the sporting goods store, I may need to learn just so I'll know what to say to people when they rent the equipment. I hope you, Emma, Amie, and I can go up to the slopes together this winter."

"That would be super fun!" Kendi agreed. "I have gone skiing with my parents several times, but I've never snowboarded. We'll have to plan a girls' weekend, and we can all learn together. Better yet, we can all hang out in the lodge together drinking mochas and sitting by the fire."

"That sounds perfect," Amie chimed in after overhearing the conversation. "Count me in!"

"Me, too!" Emma squealed, catching up to the group. "I don't even know what you are counting me in for, but don't do it without me!"

With that, all four girls giggled amongst themselves and headed for their respective rooms.

Hope knew that she was going to be too excited to sleep, so she spent some time journaling–a rare event for her–and then got drowsy, clicked off the little blue lamp next to her bed, and fell asleep.

Judy Ann Koglin

CHAPTER TWO

DTR and Doggie Date

Kendi pulled her long, red hair into a messy bun and started her early morning shift at Brandon's Coffee and Bakeshop. She was the main barista today and was having lots of fun.

Earlier in the summer, she had lobbied to add a "drink of the day", and Mark and Rachel Brandon, the owners, let her run with the idea. She had made a calendar so that whoever was behind the counter that day would know which drink to promote.

Kendi also committed to creating a beautiful sign on the shiny black dry-erase board every day with lime green and pink neon-colored markers. She was talented with drawing and lettering, so her signs always looked professional. Kendi even came in on her days off to make the sign for the next day.

Today's special was a peppermint mocha that could be served either hot or iced, and she wrote this on the board in red and white bubble letters. Yesterday's special was the almond coconut mocha, and it was also popular. However, the sound of peppermint must have appealed to a lot of customers, because Kendi felt like she was pouring the mint and chocolate syrups all day.

Kendi was also getting good at adding foam decorations on the top of the hot drinks. She loved her job.

Today, Ben, the owners' blue-eyed son, and Reed, another girl who was hired to work there during the busy season, were on duty. In between customers, the three teenagers had a chance to catch up.

"I can't believe how long your hair is getting, Ben," Reed remarked.

"I know. It always grows fast and I just let it do its thing and see what it looks like long this summer. What do you think?"

"I think you look like a surfer with your long blond hair," Reed commented. "Or, maybe a hippie," she laughed.

"How 'bout you, Kendi?" he asked expectantly.

Kendi, always the diplomat, answered carefully. "Well, what do *you* think of it?"

Ben shrugged. "I kinda like it," he admitted.

"Well, that's what matters," Kendi stated. "I actually like it, too."

Changing the subject, Ben turned towards Reed. "Hey, Reed, have I been seeing you around town with Hannah's boyfriend's brother?" Ben asked. "I can't remember his name."

"Drew?" Reed replied innocently.

Ben nodded. "Yeah, Drew. Are you dating?"

"Um, maybe… we've gone to a few things together. We haven't had a DTR," Reed answered.

"A what?" Kendi asked, having only heard part of the conversation.

"A DTR…you know, a 'define the relationship' conversation," Ben explained. "Reed and Drew haven't had it yet."

"Oh, yeah, I saw you together at the diner with Hannah and Evan," Kendi commented. "You look cute together!"

Reed whirled around quickly, her shiny, jet black hair swinging behind her, and almost ran back to the kitchen.

"Oh, no, what did I say?" Kendi asked helplessly.

"I think she is just embarrassed," Ben shrugged. Changing the subject, he asked Kendi, "Have you had a DTR talk before?"

"Um, no. I've never been in that position yet," Kendi admitted. "Have you?"

"A couple times. I guess I can sometimes be a little too friendly or flirty and make girls think I'm interested in them when I don't mean to give off that impression. It's awkward to have that friend-zoning conversation."

Kendi's heart sank a little. That was exactly the kind of vibe he gave off. Both she and Emma had wondered all summer if he was interested in one of them. He was so hard to read.

Kendi decided to say something bolder than she normally would. "How does a girl know if you are actually interested in her if you act that way with everybody?" She paused, waiting to see what he would say.

He shrugged when he looked at her and confessed, "I dunno. I go to the formal dances with girls, but I've never really dated anyone outside of that. Flirting is my comfort zone, and I've never really wanted anything beyond that..."

Kendi's heart pounded in her chest and she half expected Ben to finish with "until now," but he remained silent. She chastised herself sternly for being like all the other girls and reading too much into Ben's constant friendliness. Kendi resolved not to make that same mistake again going forward.

She stepped away and said brusquely, "Well, I'm sure when the time is right, it'll all fall into place. I'm going to go check on Reed."

Just as Kendi was about to head to the back, Reed re-emerged through the floppy door that separated the kitchen from the front of the shop.

"Hey, Reed, I'm sorry if my comment upset you." Kendi started.

"Oh, no, not at all! I just had to pee," she laughed.

"Oh, good. We thought we might have teased you too much about Drew," Ben responded.

"No, go ahead and tease me! I'm glad I finally *have* someone to be teased about," Reed admitted.

"Well, he seems like a good guy," Ben surmised. "Maybe you can take him to homecoming and go to his in Wenatchee."

"Slow your roll, Ben! We aren't even official yet!" Reed protested.

"Never hurts to look ahead," Ben said with a wink. "Kendi and I are both looking to you for relationship advice."

"You're crazy!" Reed gave them a puzzled look, grabbed her phone, and headed toward the door. "Hey, it's already past two o'clock. I gotta bounce. My dad and I are going into town to look for a car. Just wait 'til you see what I drive up in tomorrow!"

19

"Have fun!" Kendi called after her. She grabbed a bottle of Windex and a roll of paper towels and busied herself cleaning the front door and hoped to avoid an uncomfortable conversation with Ben. She wondered if Ben had intentionally worded his comment to Reed to make it sound like she and Ben were in a relationship. *That was weird.*

Just then, she saw an attractive couple with a white dog walking towards the front door. She had met them earlier this summer in the park and again when they had come by to get coffee. The couple tied the dog's leash securely to the stop sign pole, and Kendi held the door open for them.

"Hi Christopher and Lynsie!" Kendi greeted them warmly. "Hi, Duke!" she called to their cute doggie in a sweet voice and was greeted with some eager panting and a wild tail wag.

"Hi, Kendi!" Lynsie and Christopher chorused.

"Have you recovered from the robbery?" Christopher asked as they approached the counter.

Kendi reflected back to earlier that summer when an armed man entered the store one morning and pulled his gun on the coffee shop filled with customers, including Christopher and Lynsie. Emma had stopped by to get coffee on her way to work that day, and Kendi was manning the cash register and they had to face the gunman directly.

20

Nobody was hurt, and the police apprehended the robber before he left the store, but it was the scariest thing that Kendi had ever been through. She shuddered for a brief moment at the memory.

"Sorry," Christopher apologized. "I should not have brought that up."

"No, it's okay. Every time I remember it, I realize that each memory is less severe than the last. I think I am processing it pretty well," Kendi assured him. "How 'bout you guys?"

"Same," Lynsie replied. "I keep feeling thankful that we hadn't brought Duke that day. I think that would have complicated things quite a bit."

"I know," Christopher agreed. "The weird thing is, we always bring him on our walks. God must have been protecting him and us in some way when we left him at home that day."

"Yeah, the robber guy was pretty unhinged," Kendi agreed. "So, do you guys want to try our special of the day, or do you have something else in mind?"

"Both," Lynsie giggled. "I'll have an iced mint mocha, and Chris, do you want a hibiscus tea?"

"Yeah, hibiscus iced tea sounds awesome," Christopher replied.

Ben rang up the drinks while Kendi washed and dried her hands before making the beverages.

As Kendi was preparing their drinks, Lynsie chatted with her: "So, Kendi, we have a proposition for you. We are going to be out of town for two nights starting tomorrow visiting Christopher' s sister's new baby, and the rest of the family, of course. We wanted to bring Duke with us, but the family thought it might be better not to have an active dog around the new baby. Soooo… we were wondering if you would consider dog-sitting him? Not all day, but just before work, at lunch, after work, and before you go to bed. We would make it worth your while. Duke is pretty spoiled and used to lots of attention, so four times a day might be best. You can even spend the night in our guest room if you want."

Kendi grinned. "That sounds awesome! I would be happy to help. The only problem is that I don't have a car. How far away do you live?"

"Not a real long way," Lynsie replied, "but probably too long for your lunch break check-ins and too far to walk home alone at night. Maybe it won't work." Lynsie and Kendi both pouted.

"Maybe I can help!" Ben interjected, overhearing the conversation. "We could possibly do it together since I have a car?"

The girls both brightened at the offer.

"First, you should meet Duke," Lynsie replied. Christopher walked Ben outside to the stop sign to meet Duke, still happily secured by his leash as he contentedly watched locals and tourists pass by. The doggie, a beautiful little Maltese, jumped right up into Ben's arms and started licking his face.

"Okay, I think I passed that test!" Ben laughed at the greeting he received from Duke.

"I guess so!" Christopher agreed as they walked back into the shop. "By the way, my name is Christopher, and this is my wife Lynsie." They all shook hands.

Kendi quickly said, "This is my friend, Ben. His parents own this place."

"Wow, they missed a lot of excitement on the day you were robbed," Christopher commented.

"Yes, me too. I wish I was here instead of Kendi," Ben replied protectively, putting his arm around her.

"Yeah, but who knows? He may have seen you as more threatening, and things may have gone much worse," Lynsie chimed in. "Never know."

"True," Ben agreed as he let go of Kendi.

Kendi changed the subject, bringing the conversation back to dog-sitting: "So, let us know your address and Duke's schedule, and we can take care of everything," she promised.

Christopher wrote down his address on the back of one of the Brandon's Coffee and Bakeshop cards he had grabbed from the little plastic holder on the counter.

Ben looked at it and said, "No way, we are neighbors! You moved into the Bakers' house."

"Guilty as charged," Christopher smiled. "We moved in on June 1st."

Ben gave a nod of approval. "Our family has been so busy this summer that we haven't even been home, except after dark. That must be why we haven't seen you yet."

"I'm actually going to be teaching history and a few other classes at Chelan High this year," Christopher revealed.

"Oh, that's cool! It isn't that big of a school, so I know we'll run into each other," Ben replied.

"Do you two want to come over when you get off work, and we'll show you all of Duke's favorite things?" Christopher asked.

"Sure! We'll be done in about a half hour," Kendi replied. "Does that work for you, Ben?"

"Yep!"

"Okay, we'll see you guys after that," Lynsie responded cheerfully as they sipped their drinks and they walked out the door.

"They seem nice," Ben commented. "Where do you know them from? Just the robbery?"

"No, I'd actually met them earlier at the lake one afternoon. I asked if I could pet their dog, and we chatted. They are a really nice couple."

"Cool. Well, it will be fun to pet sit with you."

"Yeah, thanks for stepping up so I could do it. I wasn't planning to take their money," Kendi said hesitantly.

"No problem, I'm happy to just hang out with Duke…and you," Ben replied with a sparkle in his blue eyes.

Kendi sighed with exasperation. She never knew how to read him! But…he was pretty cute!

Judy Ann Koglin

CHAPTER THREE

New School for Hope

On Monday morning, Hope's mom came to town, and the two of them went to Chelan High to get Hope registered for classes.

The counselor performed an academic assessment and found that Hope was squarely in the middle of the class and would likely do fine in all the classes she wanted to take. Hope was issued a schedule, and then they went to the gym to meet Mr. Hawk, a tall man about 35 years old, who was the Athletic Director and helped with football.

Mr. Hawk's small but organized office was located right behind the gymnasium. Hope politely introduced herself and her mom Megan and told Mr. Hawk that she was going to be a transfer student in the fall and was interested in playing soccer and basketball, in addition to running track.

27

The athletic director's ears perked up, and he wanted to hear all about Hope and the sports that she was involved with back in Lynnwood. They had a good discussion, and Mr. Hawk told her that Coach Pearson was not there at the moment, but he would text her Hope's information and see if she could attend the soccer camp that started tomorrow. He asked Hope's mom a few questions about being a sports mom, and they seemed to have a good rapport.

"This year's camp runs Tuesday through Friday. You made it in here just in time. Sometimes things just work out," he said with a grin. "You'll need to get a sports physical if yours is expired. A lot of students go to Lakeside Clinic because they give the students a good deal."

Hope and Megan thanked Mr. Hawk and then headed to the clinic to see if she could walk in without an appointment. Luckily, they had an opening, and she was able to get her physical taken care of in less than an hour, well before noon.

The two of them went back to the school and turned in the paperwork to the AD's efficient-looking administrative assistant. She promised to follow up about soccer camp and ensure that Hope was contacted quickly. Before they even left the assistant's office, Hope's email app dinged an alert.

The message was from the soccer coach welcoming her to the school and the team, along with an attached form to fill out for camp. The admin had Hope forward the message to her, and she printed the permission slip and packing list right there in the office. Hope's mom read and signed the form and turned in the money for the camp which would start the following day. Hope grabbed the packing list, scanned it, and assured her mom that she had everything she needed back in her room at The Guesthouse, and she would be fine.

It was getting close to lunchtime, so Hope's mom Megan texted her brother Joe and asked him if he could break away for a quick lunch. He could, and they decided to meet at the sandwich shop. As they drove to the sandwich shop Megan commented, "Mr. Hawk is really handsome!"

"Mom, he's an old man!" Hope protested.

"Not for you, silly!"

Hope looked confused, then realization dawned on her. "Oh, you mean for *you*. I've literally never heard you talk about someone that way my whole life!"

"Well, maybe the lake breezes are helping me to loosen up a bit," Megan responded cheerfully as they parked and got out of their little old car.

"Well, I think that's great," Hope responded and gave her mom a little side-hug. At the sandwich shop, Megan and Hope sat down with Joe in a booth, and they told him how Hope was all settled with her fall schedule and was even signed up for soccer camp.

"Are you sure it is okay if I'm gone from work all week?" Hope asked.

"Of course! We'll get by just fine, and you can just work Saturday and Sunday if one of the other guys want to have the weekend off."

Hope gave a nod. "Done."

After she enjoyed a quick sandwich and a glass of lemonade, Megan remarked, "Well, I'm going to get on the road in a little while. I might explore the town a little bit before I go. I know you guys need to get back to work, so I'll say goodbye now. Hope, you're sure you don't need anything else for camp? Sunscreen or bug spray?"

"No, I have it already. We use it every day," she assured her mom.

"Okay, you make my job too easy," Megan said smiling.

"Bye, Mom!" Hope said as she hugged her.

Hope got into Uncle Joe's car to ride to work with him, and they waved goodbye to her mom.

"Maybe your mom will meet a guy to take care of her when she moves here," Joe said contemplatively.

"She doesn't need a man; she has taken care of us for years on her own," Hope declared.

"But she hasn't had a boyfriend since she was a teenager and got pregnant with you...at least not that I know of," Uncle Joe said. "She is still a very young woman. It would probably be nice for her to have a guy to take her out to dinner and just hang out with."

"I guess you're right. It's weird to think of my mom like that, but maybe she could use a friend." They pulled into the parking lot and jumped right into helping customers, and the conversation was tabled for the time being.

Judy Ann Koglin

CHAPTER FOUR

Crazy Day at Femley's

Emma was enjoying her summer in Chelan, working at Mr. Femley's General Store.

The bare minimum of people needed to run the store at any given time was three people, but usually, they had at least five or six employees working together to cover the busy summer shifts.

Ellen was the oldest lady who worked there and could be a little stern. She worked primarily at the register and was head cashier. Tricia was a woman around 50 who sometimes worked at the register, and sometimes manned the ice cream counter, but mainly stocked shelves and kept track of inventory. She was fun-loving and patient with newer staff members like Emma. Kim was Mr. Femley's daughter, and she worked weekends this summer. Her husband was a deployed soldier, and she was in town temporarily with her two boys.

Mr. Femley himself worked Monday through Friday and watched the grandchildren on the weekends so Kim could work. Ashley was a high schooler like Emma, and she worked there on weekends during the school year when the town was quiet and worked evenings during the summer. There were a couple other people who Emma didn't know very well who covered shifts there as well.

The general store had a small ice cream counter left over from the days when the store had less merchandise, but there also used to be an actual sit-down area with tables and dining chairs where people ordered ice cream and sodas. When the town grew, a stand-alone ice cream parlor was built not far from the general store. Rather than compete with the new store, the general store planned to take out their ice cream area instead. There was such an outcry from customers that they compromised by removing the seating and just scooping ice cream to go with three flavors offered on any given day, leaving more room for retail customers.

The flavors offered at the ice cream counter changed constantly, and Mr. Femley let the person who was manning the ice cream counter choose which special flavor to make when one ran out.

The only rule was that the flavor had to be creative and complex and couldn't be boring. For example, plain chocolate, strawberry, and vanilla were never allowed; customers could go to the actual ice cream store down the street if they wanted the basic flavors. The purpose of Mr. Femley's ice cream counter was crazy creativity, and the customers loved it.

Whenever Emma had the fun task of selecting a new batch of ice cream, she tried to raise the bar with unique flavors such as white licorice, lemon-passion fruit swirl, and chocolate-caramel ganache with finely crushed cookies for texture.

Today, Emma started out her shift by making a fresh batch of an innovative new flavor. She surveyed the other two remaining flavors as well as the list of flavors they had done recently. One of the current offerings had a chocolate base with almonds and biscotti chunks, and the other had a vanilla base with ribbons of caramel, chocolate, and mini chocolate chips mixed in. Emma decided they needed a fruity option and created a strawberry piña colada ice cream with pineapple and coconut flavors and chunks of strawberries and pineapple with finely grated coconut blended into the mix. She tasted her concoction and decided it was pretty darn good.

After a few hours of frozen treat work, Emma went on her lunch break. She knew they were going to be shorthanded when she got back because only three people were available to work due to various reasons. Mr. Femley had a chamber of commerce meeting, and the other employees were sick or busy, so Ellen, Tricia, and Emma would hold down the fort. Mr. Femley said that Ellen would cover the registers with Tricia as a backup, and Emma would cover the ice cream counter and help Tricia restock in between customers.

The store was unusually busy, and the three ladies were kept on their toes the whole afternoon. Emma would just get a box opened when she would hear the ding of the bell on the back counter, and she would hustle back to put on her gloves and scoop some ice cream. Tricia was kept busy behind the register most of the time so that left Emma to unload boxes and restock the rapidly emptying shelves in between her ice cream duties.

Tricia called to Emma to go to the back room to see if a new shipment of suntan oil had come in. The female customer who was trying to purchase the last bottle of it had a big leak in her bottle in Tricia's checkout line, and the yummy-smelling oil was oozing out of the bottle all over the place.

Tricia was cleaning up the mess while Ellen had a huge line of customers, and Emma was frantically opening every unmarked cardboard box in the back room that looked like it would be the right size to hold a dozen suntan oil bottles.

In the meantime, she heard the bell ring on the ice cream counter in the back and thought she'd better complete the task for Tricia's customer before heading to the ice cream area. Emma opened a couple more boxes and heard the ice cream bell ding a few more times. She finally went to the shelf and grabbed suntan oil that seemed similar to the one the customer had originally picked. She ran to the front and asked if that one would work. The customer took the other brand reluctantly, and Emma ran to the back where the bell was being rung yet again.

As she ran, she wondered who the persistent customer was. Turns out, it was eight customers: two ladies and six kids from a daycare who were evidently playing with the bell on the counter. Apparently, their outing today was a trip to Mr. Femley's General Store, and they were eager for their ice cream. Emma wished the ladies would have kept the kids from dinging the bell, but she washed her hands, put on gloves, and politely apologized for the delay and got scooping.

After she had helped all eight of them and was in the process of ringing up their purchases, she heard someone's fingers rapping insistently on the counter and a male voice saying, "Excuse me, miss, could I get some service over here?"

Emma shot the male customer a look of frustration, impatience, and friendly customer service all rolled into one flustered glare. The customer then laughed. It was Ryan Sanders, one of the cute local boys who would be a senior in the fall. He had brown hair and brown eyes and an irresistible smile, and Emma had a small crush on him all summer. He had seen that she was busy and thought he would be funny by teasing her. He didn't count on quite how overwhelmed she was at that moment, but one look at her face clued him in. Once she realized it was Ryan, and he was just teasing her, she gave him a weak smile.

Once her group of eight had paid and left the store, she asked Ryan how she could help. He ordered an ice cream and apologized for pretending to be an irate customer. He said he would make it up to her by getting her a coffee.

"Thanks, but I don't have time to drink anything. It's too crazy today."

"When do you get off work?"

"At five," Emma replied.

"Okay," Ryan looked at the time on his phone. "I'll meet you at Brandon's at 5:05, and I'll get you that coffee."

Emma wanted to protest that he didn't have to do that, but she wasn't going to blow the chance to spend time with one of the handsomest guys who had ever talked to her.

"Okay! I'll see ya there!" Emma agreed.

Suddenly, she was on top of the world, and her shift at work was awesome. She practically danced through the aisles as she helped customers, did price checks for the cashiers, and stocked the shelves. It eventually slowed down enough for Tricia to leave the registers and stock shelves with Emma. They laughed at the spilled suntan oil and the group of eight ice cream cones in the middle of all the chaos.

Tricia mentioned that Emma seemed awfully chipper. "Did I happen to see Ryan Sanders in the store earlier? Is that why you are in such a good mood?"

Emma's dark eyes sparkled. "He may or may not be buying me a coffee when I get off work,"

"Oooooo, Emma's got a date!" Tricia chirped.

"Not exactly a date, but maybe this will lead to a real date," Emma commented happily.

Just then, Mr. Femley came in the door. The store was completely quiet with only two customers in the whole place, belying the chaos of the last few hours.

"It looks like you girls had a slow afternoon," he commented.

Tricia and Emma burst out laughing, and Ellen threw a lime-colored novelty koosh ball at him.

The three of them filled in Mr. Femley about the day's events, and he stated that he and Ashley must have dodged a bullet.

Just then, the tinkle of bells sounded as the glass front door opened and Ashley walked in to begin her evening shift. Emma gave her a brief synopsis of the day, and Tricia reviewed what still needed to be done with the new product shipments.

While she would have loved to stay a little later to help Ashley, Emma had a coffee date with a tall, dark, and handsome boy, so promptly at five, she clocked out, grabbed her stuff from the break room, and took off for the coffee shop.

CHAPTER FIVE

Soccer Camp

The next morning, Aunty Nola brought Hope to the school parking lot bright and early to board the bus for team camp. Hope thanked Aunty Nola for the ride and gave her a quick hug before joining her new team.

Sierra, a girl she had met while running earlier this summer, pulled up and got out of her car. about the same time Hope was walking to the bus.

"Don't tell me I talked you into moving here?" Sierra teased.

"Actually, I *am* staying here after all! I just signed up for school yesterday, and I'm coming to camp."

"Oh, that is so great, Hope! You'll love it here."

"I already do," Hope admitted.

Sierra then pointed out, "There's Coach Pearson now."

A pretty, athletic woman with a clipboard walked up to them. "You must be Hope Stevens! Welcome to Chelan High and the soccer team. I'm Coach Pearson. When we get on the road, I'll introduce you to the team. Coach Anderson will meet us there."

Hope and Sierra boarded the bus and found seats towards the back. Sierra introduced her to a few of the other players: Amber, Celeste, and Alyssa. They chatted a little while about her team back in Lynnwood. It reminded Hope that she would probably need to tell her other team that she was moving and going to a new school. She thought she'd better wait to send the text since it was barely seven in the morning. Coach Pearson kept looking at her watch and peering out the front window.

"Who are we waiting for?" Hope asked.

"We are waiting for Jonna," Amber explained. "She is always late because she always needs to have her hair and makeup perfect–even if she is going on a bus at seven in the morning with a bunch of other girls–and we're going to a camp with no boys within a mile of the soccer fields."

The motor started, and the girls looked up and saw a beautiful girl wearing too much makeup, slightly out of breath, climbing up the bus steps.

She looked like she was headed to a photo shoot instead of a soccer camp, in Hope's opinion. *So, this is Jonna,* Hope thought.

As if reading Hope's thoughts, Celeste muttered, "She might not look like it, but she is a great player, so Coach puts up with her."

"Is she nice?" Hope asked.

"Yeah, she's fine," Alyssa replied in hushed tones while Jonna found a seat. "Just a little too concerned about how she looks in my opinion."

The bus started up, and they were on the road. About two miles out of town, Coach Pearson got up to make some announcements. "First of all, let's welcome our newest team member, Hope Stevens. As you know, we have been needing to fill the roster, so Hope showing up was an answer to prayer. She is a junior from Lynnwood High near Seattle, and she has had a lot of varsity playing time as a sophomore, so she should be able to hit the ground running with us, so to speak. It looks like several of you have already met her.

"So, about camp this week," she continued. "As those of you who have been there before know, we will be staying at a college campus. The dorms are broken into quads. I've assigned you to a roommate, and there's no use asking me nor Coach Anderson to make a change…it ain't happening.

Basically, you will only be there long enough to sleep anyway. On the field, we will be trying out everyone in different positions than you are used to. No whining! We want to see how flexible you are and how well you can roll with something new. And remember, the leaders of the camp give out a sportsmanship award and an MVP award for each team. The Chelan coaches do not select the winners, the camp leadership does. At the end of camp, each team is competing for a sportsmanship trophy by school. Nothing would thrill us coaches more that if we take home that trophy. Well…that one, in addition to the championship team trophy. Let's see if we can get both!"

Her speech fell on deaf ears as most of the girls had fallen asleep due to getting up earlier than usual to be on the bus before seven. Hope decided to close her eyes too, and she, too, soon dozed off.

****

When they arrived at camp, they got their bunk assignments: Hope was sharing a room with Sierra, and they were combined in a quad with Celeste and Jonna, who would both be juniors in the fall. Hope was relieved that she was with someone she already knew. Before they went to their rooms, they were given packets that included lanyards and ID badges that doubled as electronic keys.

They were also given a map and a printed schedule and told to go put their stuff in their dorms, get in their uniforms, and come down to lunch. Hope put on the practice uniform that Coach Pearson had brought for her. Fortunately, their dorm was located near the dining hall and not far from the practice fields.

Sierra and Hope scrutinized their schedules while they had lunch in the dining hall. They had passing and shooting drills in early afternoon with their own coaches, and then they would combine with a few other teams and run the drills competitively. Later in the day, they were scheduled to separate from their teammates and go into groups with other girls who played their position for specific training.

Celeste and Jonna had gotten their food and sat across from Sierra and Hope.

"What position do you play, Hope?" Jonna asked.

"Um, I can play any position that's needed." Hope used her standard line because she didn't want to step on anyone's toes. "What about all of you?"

"I play midfield with Sierra. Alyssa is a goalie, and Amber and Celeste are backs. They might put you in forward. Can you score goals?"

"Yes," Hope confirmed. She started to tell them of the success she had playing forward on her 4A varsity team back home, but she bit her tongue and decided to let her playing do the talking.

The four girls finished their lunch and headed to the practice area that was assigned to their team.

During the first passing drill, a coach from the college that was hosting the camp came by and watched the girls' technique. The coach offered helpful suggestions and, although Hope was already a good ball handler, she was pleased to see that she was learning new skills. It felt good for her to be back on the field. All year long, she ran mainly for fitness, not for fun, but she played soccer because she absolutely loved it. She and Sierra also played well together, which certainly helped.

After a while, Sierra called over to her, "I'm glad I talked you into staying in town!"

One of the college coaches introduced the Chelan girls and coaches to Mindi Alton, a nationally recognized college soccer player who would be the Chelan girls' mentor during camp. Hope was already a fan of Mindi's because her coach from Lynnwood had game film of some of Mindi's games that he instructed the Lynnwood High team to study.

Mindi was a slim, tan girl with a platinum blonde bob and a big smile. Hope was struck by how similar she looked to her roommate Amie, except that Mindi was about seven inches taller. The coaches explained that Mindi was there to give them tips regarding soccer skills, but she was also there just to talk if anyone had questions about teamwork, fitness routines, stretching, etc.

Pretty soon, it was time to switch to the next rotation where they competed with other teams from different schools and towns on different events such as dribbling relays, shooting on a goalie from one of the other teams, and dribbling against opponents. The Chelan team did well in all areas, and their coaches and Mindi were pleased.

Afterwards, the team gathered around Mindi and their coaches and were told which position group they were attending for specific training. As expected, the coaches sent Hope off to the striker group, a position near the other team's goalie.

Coach Pearson pulled Hope aside before she released them and said that she was going to have her go to the midfielder group on the next rotation. This was a surprise to Hope since she always played striker in the past, but she nodded and jogged off to the area on the field where the strikers were receiving instruction for the first session.

Hope found that this session was really informative. They had NCAA women's soccer players teach the sessions. It was fun to have college athletes that Hope had actually heard of teaching her personally. She wanted to ask for their autograph, especially Mindi's, but she didn't want to bother them.

After an hour of training in this position, individual teams converged again, and the coaches told their girls which station to go to next.

Hope was sent to the midfielder group with Jonna. Sierra, who had been at the midfielder station the first time, was sent to the goalies. Hope enjoyed the athletes who taught this session and learned a lot about the expectations and strategies of this position. She had never especially wanted to play in this role but hearing the college athletes talk about the importance of it partially changed her mind.

Hope got to spend time talking with Jonna during this rotation and found that she seemed fairly nice, although she made it clear that there were people on the team with established positions, and Hope would need to respect that. Hope tried to imagine if the roles were reversed, she was back on her team in Lynnwood, Jonna had moved to her school, and showed up at her camp.

Would I act that way? she thought with a shrug, honestly unsure if she would be so unwelcoming.

Before coming to camp, Hope had wondered how her new teammates would treat her. Would they be territorial, or would they welcome her with open arms? There seemed to be a mix of this on the Chelan team. To her, it felt like they were glad to have another strong player, but nobody wanted her to play their position, and they didn't want another player to compete for the MVP trophy.

Hope reeled in her thoughts and focused on the teaching. Since she had rarely played midfield, she learned a lot about that position.

When the session was over and the girls converged with their own teams again, they were told that they were going to go back to their dorms, get cleaned up and go to dinner, and then meet in the gym for an all-camp skills training. The college athletes were going to demonstrate skills while one of the college coaches talked them through strategy. Hope was really looking forward to learning what they had to teach tonight.

At dinner, Hope and Sierra sat with Amber and Alyssa. Earlier in the day, Amber had twisted her ankle during one of the rotations, but she said it wasn't too bad and wanted to play on it during the tournament that started tomorrow afternoon.

Coach Anderson and Pearson wrapped her ankle and agreed to let her rest it so she could possibly be ready to compete in the later rounds of the tournament, assuming they got that far.

After dinner, the girls grabbed their notebooks and headed to the massive gym for the demonstrations.

Hope was awed by the talent level of the college players and their ball-handling skills. She took a lot of notes and listened attentively to what their coach was saying. Hope was excited to try out some of the moves she was learning and hoped that the other girls were feeling the same way. When she looked around, though, she saw that some of her teammates, including Sierra, looked bored. Some of the girls were stealing glances at their phones, and only a few seemed to be focused on the presentation. Jonna was one of the focused ones; she had taken as many notes as Hope and really seemed intent at improving her skills.

They had asked for a few volunteers from the audience to come down and try an interchange they just talked about. About half of the girls in the stands raised their hands. They randomly selected three girls with their hands up from different teams. Sierra was one of the girls selected to demonstrate the skills that they just learned.

Unfortunately, Sierra had not been paying enough attention during the instruction, and the college coach had to explain the drill to her over the microphone to her red-faced embarrassment. The coach used her as an example and told the audience that their parents had paid a lot of money to come to camp and to play soccer in general, and the way to pay back that investment was to make the most of the learning provided.

Sierra was a good athlete, and once the drill was explained to her, she was able to execute it well. All three of the girls did a good job, and the coach patted each of them on the back as she sent them back to their places on the bleachers.

Once the coach was finished with the session, the camp director took the microphone and explained how tomorrow would go. It would be a full day with drills in the morning for each individual team led by assigned college athletes. In the afternoon, the single-elimination tournament would start. Once each team was eliminated, they would go back to their area and could either do drills or a scrimmage against members of their own team, whichever their respective coaches determined would be more beneficial. When the games were over for the day, they would have dinner followed by another gym session led by the college coaches.

This would be the same schedule for Thursday as well. On the last morning, they would all gather in the stadium to watch the championship game and give out the trophies.

Coach Pearson and Coach Anderson huddled with their team before letting them leave the gym. Coach Anderson said that they had a good shot in this tournament and wanted everyone to play with the mentality that they were going to win the tournament–no daydreaming–and every move had to be intentional and precise.

She asked the girls if they wanted to play soccer games for the rest of camp or go back to doing drills.

The girls chorused, "Soccer games!"

"Well, okay," Coach Anderson admonished, "this can happen if you keep your head in the games. Otherwise, we will be back on our section of the practice field doing drill after drill. You girls have the talent to win all these games…I just don't know if you have the mental toughness. Get some good rest tonight, and we'll see you at breakfast tomorrow."

The girls chatted excitedly about the tournament as they walked back to their dorm rooms. Sierra and Celeste were the team captains, and they sternly told the other girls to play well tomorrow.

They did NOT want to be eliminated and have to do drills all day tomorrow, so everyone needed to bring their A game so they could advance in the tournament. Their teammates all agreed.

****

At some point during the evening, the circuit that powered the outlet that Sierra and Hope were using to charge their phones had a malfunction, and both Sierra's and Hope's phones didn't charge. By morning, both their phones had died so their alarms did not go off, and they overslept.

Luckily, Celeste and Jonna were in an argument about the shared bathroom that became so loud that it woke Sierra and Hope up. That gave them enough time for lightning-quick showers, dressing, and running out the door to breakfast.

The coach wanted a team picture out on the field, so they headed out there first. Coach Anderson mentioned that all the girls looked like they hadn't slept all night and hoped that wasn't the case.

The girls ran some warm-up drills, then jogged to the field where their first game would be played. Their first opponent turned out to be stiff competition. Coach Pearson gave them a rousing pep talk prior to the game, which revved them all up to play their best. Hope played in the striker position and scored the first of their two goals.

With Amber out with an injury, the coach had to put one of the sophomore girls who barely played on varsity in her position. The poor girl was not ready to play at this level, and she let a lot of balls pass by which made Alyssa have to work even harder at goalie but she stepped up to the challenge and played well. In the end, the Chelan girls won the first round, displacing a good opponent from the tournament.

For the next game, the coaches wanted to put Amber back in, but they felt that they needed to let her rest her ankle a little more. To give Amber a fair chance to rest, they decided to put Hope in as a back to help defend the goal. Hope was disappointed to move from her striker position, and she was worried about if she would do okay in this other role, but she wanted to show that she was a team player so she accepted the role with a smile.

The team they played this time was mostly comprised of younger players and it was not as strong as their last opponent, so the Chelan girls were able to win easily. Hope enjoyed being in the back with Celeste and Alyssa and matched their intensity. They did not allow a single score this game. Hope like playing this defensive position and hoped she would play it again.

For the next game, Hope got her wish and played in the back with Celeste and Alyssa again. The team played remarkably well together, and for the third time in a row, won the victory.

They proudly made their way to the dining hall for lunch. Hope joined Sierra, Celeste, and Jonna for the walk. Sierra was telling them about a funny prank that Bryan and his friends played at football camp. The girls all laughed hysterically. Hope had walked up ahead and was trying to catch up to Alyssa to talk about how the last game went, but Alyssa and Amber were deep in conversation.

"I don't care where she came from, she doesn't get to take my position away from me," Amber retorted with a flounce.

"I was just saying that the team could use another strong player—not in your spot," Alyssa protested.

"Interesting that this conversation came up immediately after she played my position the last two games," Amber snarked. "I'm telling Coach that my ankle is better and that I am ready to get back in there before she permanently takes my position!"

Hope felt herself get red in the face and hoped no one would notice. She drew back pretended to tie her shoe as she waited for Sierra's group to pass.

She walked alone and silently reflected, *I didn't expect to be welcomed to the team like a long-awaited hero, but I also didn't want girls to be mad at me and consider me a threat. I have a hard-enough time making friends as it is without starting on the wrong foot with my teammates.*

She considered approaching Amber directly to try to sort things out, but she decided to let the tournament play out to decide whether she should make a move. She felt sick from the conversation she overheard and barely touched her lunch.

They were scheduled to have two more games today, and then they would have the all-group training in the gym tonight. Tomorrow would be another day like today, and the championship game would be played Sunday morning, followed by the awards ceremony before they loaded the buses to go home.

During lunch, Hope saw Amber talking to Coach Pearson. Amber seemed to be trying to persuade her coach to let her do something. Hope was pretty sure she was trying to get permission to resume her regular position on defense. Hope was not able to ascertain what kind of answer the coach gave her, because neither of them gave a clue from their facial expressions.

After lunch, the Chelan team headed to their field for their game. Coach Anderson pulled Hope aside and told her that they were transitioning Amber back in and Hope and Amber would rotate quarters in the back so Amber's ankle could rest.

"We might get you in for a quarter in striker, too," Coach Anderson mentioned. "You are doing a great job, Hope."

Buoyed by the coach's praise, Hope took her place on the sideline.

Mindi Alton came up to her and said, "Hey, Hope, I heard you were just a junior. Is that right?"

"Yes, I'll be a junior this year," Hope replied.

"I hope you are thinking of playing college soccer. Are you?" Mindi asked.

"Yes, I would really like to but a scholarship is the only way I'll get to college," Hope replied.

"I suspect you will get more than one offer," Mindi assured her. "Find me on social media! I'd love to keep in touch."

"I'll do that! Thank you for the encouragement."

"No problem! You'll do great in whatever position you play. Hope, there will always be haters who get mad at your success. Don't let them get to you. Let your light shine, but always be kind to the other players." With that, Mindi took off to find a place in the stands.

Hope thought about what she had said. She wondered if others were talking behind her back, and Mindi knew about it. There was no time to dwell on it because the game was starting.

Amber and Hope traded off positions, and they both played well. Chelan won both of the games they played by a good margin.

The team was on cloud nine as they went in for dinner and to the gym afterwards. The lesson tonight centered on teamwork, both on the field and off. Two former college players, who now played soccer professionally, came up to the front to tell their story.

The shorter girl talked first. "I was an all-state player in high school, and I went to the University of Washington on a full scholarship and was their starting goalie as a freshman. In my junior year, another hotshot goalie transferred in from a community college," she added, pointing to the taller brunette. "Now, I had some real competition and had to defend my position. Sometimes, competition can be healthy, but in this case, it was not. We were both fighting so hard for the position that we lost sight of what was best for the team. We never fought with words, but we were icy whenever we were around each other, and our silent feud was very detrimental to the whole team.

It got so bad that we ended up both getting benched for a game. Our coach had to have a meeting with us to knock us from our pedestals."

The taller girl then took up the story: "We both thought we were da bomb, and we both thought that there was only room for one goalie on the team. Our coach made us see that having two goalies was a great thing because we could help each other at practice, we could sub in for each other in games and always be fresh and rested, we could have a special partner on the sidelines who could see things we didn't see, et cetera. The list of positives far outweighed the negatives.

"Once we saw that," the first girl jumped back in, "we grew in respect for each other and appreciated the strengths of the other person. We even became good friends. None of this would have happened if we didn't do a couple things. One, we had to realize that we were not 'all that.' It is easy to think you are when you are an elite athlete, but there is always someone out there better than you, and if you are not humble in the first place, you will be humbled by someone else eventually. And two, we had to realize that we were just a cog in the wheel of our soccer team. We are an important part of the team, but so is everyone else. If everyone isn't doing their job, we all suffer."

The coach came to the mic and wrapped up.

Hope had listened to the talk carefully. The girls who spoke tonight were amazing professional soccer players and knew what they were talking about. Hope knew she could learn more from them. She also thought of the conversation she had overheard earlier and pondered how she could be a better teammate and convince Amber that she wasn't there to steal her position.

She joined Sierra, Celeste, and Jonna as they walked back to their room. The other girls were brimming with excitement for the championship game. They chatted away about how they were going to stand in the picture if they won the trophy and wondered how tough the other team was going to be. Despite her sadness earlier, Hope felt a lot better now, and she was glad to be part of this team.

Hope took a minute to reflect about the talk she had with Mindi. It was as if she knew what was going on with Amber. Hope shrugged and thought, *Maybe it was just a coincidence.* She stretched out on her bed and, as she drifted off to sleep, she thought about Aunty Nola, of all people. Hope wondered how she would handle the Amber situation if she was a teenager on this soccer team. Hope smiled at her own imagination.

CHAPTER SIX

Emma's Coffee Date

Emma showed up at Brandon's Coffee and Bakeshop promptly at 5:05, just as Ryan pulled up in his car. They walked in together. Reed and Lynn, a middle-aged lady who Emma often saw working in and out of the kitchen, seemed to be the only people working. They approached the counter where the black sign said: "Today's Special Cinnamon-Vanilla Latte – Iced or Hot."

Emma said, "I'll take the special please."

"Hot or iced?" Lynn asked.

"Iced."

"Make that two, also iced." Ryan agreed, pulling out his debit card. He paid for both the drinks, and moments later, Reed handed them to Emma and Ryan.

Emma sat down at a table near the window, and Ryan followed.

"Sorry for frazzling you earlier," Ryan apologized with a grin.

"You made up for it. Coffee is my love language," Emma reassured him. "This one is especially yummy. I tend to get in a rut with my iced mochas, so it is fun to try the specials here."

"I know this one is pretty good." Ryan took a sip, to confirm his statement, and his grin was evidence.

"So, how do you happen to be in town?" Emma couldn't help but ask. "I thought you were busy at Slip and Slide every day."

Ryan smiled. "I'm not the only one who works at the water park. Even assistant managers get to take time off sometimes."

"Oh yeah, that makes sense." Emma mentally kicked herself for her naïve comment. She tried to think of something better to say. Ryan saved her.

"So, Emma, tell me about your family's winery."

"Well," Emma began, "my grandparents and my parents started it together when my parents were fresh out of college. My dad works for Hanford in Richland, and my mom is an attorney and works at the prosecutor's office in Pasco, but everyone works hard during harvest time in the fall."

"So, Richland and Pasco are two of the three cities in the Tri-Cities. What is the other one?"

"Kennewick. Kennewick is the largest of the three. It has Costco and the mall and is more of the retail center. Pasco has more of the agriculture, and it has the airport. North Richland is considered a research district and has a lot of businesses that support science. There is a huge lab out there that researches all kinds of things like national security, the environment, longer battery life, and microscopic particles. I have toured it before with my school, and it is incredible, but Pasco is the best. That is where we live, and that is where we have the winery."

"Do you have a tasting room at the winery?"

"Yes! My grandma and grandpa run the tasting room most of the time because my parents are at work, but sometimes, my parents get involved, like when they host big functions in the event room. The room is really big and beautiful and overlooks the valley. We do lots of weddings, quinceañeras, and corporate events."

"Wow, that sounds awesome! I've never been to the Tri-Cities before, but if we ever go down that way, we'll have to come check it out."

"That would be fun. I could give you a tour," Emma said proudly.

"Do you crush the grapes with your feet?" Ryan asked, eyes wide. "I saw someone do that on TV."

"Well, we have before, but now we have machinery that does it. It is pretty fun to do a crush, though."

Ryan took another sip of iced coffee before asking, "You have the Columbia River where you live, too, right?"

"Yes, and the Snake River. That is something I have really missed this summer, going on the river with my family. We tend to go on the Snake more often than the Columbia because it is warmer. My sister and I like to ride on inner tubes behind the boat. I've always been afraid to ski and wakeboard, but I love tubing."

"It must be hard for you to be away from home for so long."

Emma shrugged. "It hasn't been too bad. I saw them when they dropped me off, then they came on the Fourth of July and again on the day after the robbery. We Facetime a lot. I have great parents."

"Have you enjoyed your summer here?" Ryan asked with genuine interest.

"Definitely. The scenery is beautiful, and the people are so nice. Not only that, but I also became a Christian here and met great friends. It has been an amazing summer so far."

"Well, good. I'm glad you've had a great summer. Chelan is a special place. I'm grateful that I got to grow up in a place where people wait all year just to spend a week."

"What's next for you?" Emma inquired.

"Well, senior year, I guess. I'm student body president this year, so I'll be busy with that. I'm thinking of trying out for one of the school plays, too. I'll take the SAT, get senior pictures, go to football games, do college visits, and take a full load of AP classes, so I'll be pretty slammed."

Emma let out a sigh. "Wow, that makes me tired just thinking of all of that. I'm glad I'm just a junior. Do you play any sports?"

"No. I did when I was younger, but there are enough athletic guys in our class that I never really pursued any school sports. I worked at the water park a lot, too, so not a lot of extra time, at least not in the fall. Don't feel sorry for me...I wasn't slave labor. I actually got paid pretty well for a kid."

"Are you a saver or spender?" Emma asked, the gears in her business-minded brain turning.

"Well, I give a tithe to the church first, and then I usually put half in savings and keep half for spending."

"That's such a good plan," Emma remarked. "I think I will do something like that."

"Yeah, it works out well so you can build your savings but still be able to have some instant gratification, too."

"A tithe is 10%, right?" Emma asked.

"Yes, traditionally. But the new testament says everyone can determine what they want to give, and God wants us to give cheerfully and not out of obligation. Some people give more and some people give less," he shrugged.

"What do you plan to do after high school?"

"College for sure, but I'm not sure where yet. I'll probably go on visits this fall. I like Western and UW, but I don't like the rain, so I'll probably stick to the east side of the state, possibly WSU or Eastern. How about you?"

"I think I will probably end up at WSU. It is only two hours from my house and has a good business program…but we'll see. I still have lots of time to decide. Where I live, we have a huge junior college. A lot of kids take college classes that count for high school credit so they can knock out two years of college for free while in high school. I didn't sign up for it this year, but maybe I'll do it next year. Then, my parents will only have to pay for three years at WSU."

"There is a WSU branch campus in the Tri-Cities too, isn't there?"

"Yes, it's a pretty good option as well. If I went there, I wouldn't have to move away from home. But, by then, maybe I will be ready to spread my wings a little…who knows? What major are you going to choose?"

"I haven't decided. Possibly management or finance. My dad works for a college besides owning the water park with my mom. The water park is his fun business, but he has his hand in several other endeavors, and I have learned a lot being around during some of his meetings with investors, lawyers, et cetera. I might study business in undergrad and then go on to law school."

"Wow, that will set you up for success," Emma responded.

"Yeah, it would be nice to chat with your mom sometime when she is back in town."

"She would love that! She always encourages people to go to law school. She won't be back until they pick me up to go home, though."

"That's okay. It is a long time before I have to decide about going to law school." Just then, Ryan got a loud text alert and looked down at his phone. "Oh, that's my mom. I totally forgot that we were meeting my grandpa and grandma for dinner tonight at Stillwaters. It's my grandpa's birthday. I'd better get over there."

"Oh, totally," Emma agreed, standing. "Thank you so much for the coffee. I enjoyed hanging out with you."

"You too," Ryan replied, typing in a hurried text to his mom then hustling out the front door. "See you later!"

CHAPTER SEVEN

Championship Game

Two mornings later, Hope was awakened by the sound of "We are the Champions" by Queen blasting on Jonna's Bluetooth speaker. The girls were dancing around excitedly in their pajamas, and Hope couldn't help but catch their enthusiasm. The girls were hyped after another day of victories that advanced them to the championship game.

"Maybe we should hold off on playing that song until after we actually win," Hope suggested.

Jonna must have agreed, because she changed the song, and soon, "The Final Countdown was blasting in their room as they got ready.

The girls went down the stairs of the dorm and entered the dining hall. Sierra headed over to the tables where the rest of the team was sitting and sat down across from Amber and Alyssa.

Hope still had not resolved things with Amber, but she decided she would take the high road. She sat down next to Sierra and said, "Hey, guys! Ready for today?"

"Absolutely!" Alyssa said.

Amber nodded in agreement. "I'm totally psyched that my ankle is better and I can play my position the whole game," she added, looking Hope in the eye.

"That's awesome," Hope agreed. "You did great yesterday. No one would have guessed that you had a twisted ankle."

"Thanks," Amber replied with a smile that felt genuine. "Hopefully today's game will go just as well."

Hope was relieved that Amber was cordial to her, and they finished their breakfast listening to Sierra and Alyssa recount a funny story about a prank some of the senior girls played on Coach Pearson a few years ago.

Sierra ended the story by saying, "It's a good thing Coach had a sense of humor, or those girls would have been SO in trouble!"

Hope observed that the dining hall was quickly emptying and said, "We probably need to get moving."

The teammates got up and walked toward the indoor arena where the championship game would be played.

They did some warm-up drills on the field, and Coach Pearson huddled them up and talked strategy. "This team is strong in their offense but less strong in their defense. I think we have a good chance at getting some early goals, but we really need our A game on defense. Alyssa, Celeste, Amber, are you all healthy?"

The three girls nodded enthusiastically.

"How's the ankle, Amber?" Coach Anderson looked her in the eye.

"It's 100%, coach."

"Okay," said Coach Anderson. "We'll let you play back there, but if it is bothering you, we will need to sub you out."

Amber nodded in response.

"Hope, we'll put you back on offense," Coach Pearson said. "Let's see if we can put a couple points on the board early on."

Mindi Alton then spoke briefly about how proud she was of this team making it to the championship game and told them she would be cheering them on from the stands. "Remember, focus on your passing game, girls. That is where the game is won."

The game started, and Hope was in the zone. After a play that comprised of about 13 well-executed passes between six of her teammates, she was able to score an early point. Her teammates gathered around and gave each other high fives.

The other team took possession of the ball, and it seemed for a moment that they were going to do the same thing. Fortunately, Celeste was able to go in for a steal, recovered possession of the ball, and passed it up to one of the midfielders who worked it around to other teammates. One of the girls took a shot and barely missed, the ball hitting the goal post and ricocheting out of bounds.

There were several more good plays by Chelan, both on offense and defense, but the score remained 1-0 until the last quarter.

The striker on the other team was able to take a shot, which Alyssa dove for heroically, but missed, tying the game at 1-1 with five minutes remaining.

At that point, the team huddled, and Coach Pearson said they were too close not to bring home the Camp Trophy, so they needed to get fierce.

When the huddle broke, Chelan mounted a great passing offense that culminated with Sierra scoring a spectacular goal with 30 seconds left in the game. The girls ran to the center and hugged it out.

The other team tried to match this point, but they came up short, and Chelan won the tournament.

****

At the awards ceremony, a prize was given to a member of each team for sportsmanship. This award was given to Celeste and all her teammates agreed that she was a good choice.

The team MVP was given to Sierra for her on-the-field leadership as well as for scoring the winning goal, and the girls seemed to agree with that as well.

It was then announced that Chelan had won the tournament championship game, which most teams had already heard. The ceremony emcees said to wait on coming down to the field for pictures until the last award was announced.

The camp director came up to the microphone and said that the sportsmanship award was the result of watching teams over the course of camp and taking notes on what they had observed. "It was a close decision," said the director, "but we tallied up all the observations, and this year's team sportsmanship award also goes to Chelan High! It was a pleasure to watch you girls play. You passed well and seemed to genuinely care about your teammates. Let's give it up for Chelan High!"

The other teams clapped politely, while Hope reflected briefly on the award. She wasn't entirely sure they deserved it, but, for the most part, she felt welcomed and appreciated by the team. Not only that, but the girls on the sidelines were also vocal supporters of the girls who were on the field, so maybe the award was warranted. The team excitedly hurried down to the field for pictures.

The celebration after the game was nothing short of euphoric with everyone passing the trophy around for photos and reliving every moment. It was as if they'd won a state championship game instead of just a camp tournament.

For the girls, it was a promise of a great season to come. Hope got more hugs and congratulations after the game than she had ever gotten before in a whole year!

After their celebration, the girls went back and grabbed their luggage.

As they reached the bus, their mentor Mindi Alton came up and hugged each girl as they boarded. She whispered to Hope, "You WILL play college soccer. I'm not kidding about what I said earlier. Please look me up on social media, I want to keep in touch. Actually, let me have your phone." Mindi then added her contact info to Hope's phone.

Hope grinned under the compliment from her new mentor and promised to keep in touch. As she got on the bus, Hope sent an initial text to Mindi to thank her for all the encouragement and Mindi replied with a smile, a heart, and a soccer ball emoji. The bus ride was really loud and fun, and the coaches took turns giving short speeches along the way.

****

When they arrived back to the parking lot, several cars were waiting. Some of the girls had posted pictures of the team with the trophy on social media already, and people had come to congratulate them. Even though Sierra was in the back of the bus, she darted to the front and was the first one off. She dove into the waiting arms of her boyfriend Bryan, and he swung her around a few times and gave her a kiss. All the girls watched from the bus windows and gave whistles and "Whoos" to the couple.

"Hashtag couple goals," Amber remarked.

The other girls filed out and were met by parents and friends. Hope hadn't made any arrangements for a pickup, and Celeste asked if she needed a ride home.

"Oh thanks, that would be great…" Hope began.

She was interrupted by Conner who came up behind her and grabbed her waist. "Hey, girls! I hear congratulations are in order?"

Celeste and a few other girls who were still around laughed. "Yes, they are!"

He high fived all the girls. "Championship trophy AND team trophy. Double winners. Way to represent!"

"And it looks like you have met our new player already," Celeste commented.

Conner nodded. "I have. I'm so glad she is going to stick around this year."

"We are too, obviously," Celeste agreed with Conner. "Hope, it looks like you won't need that ride home after all."

"Yeah, I can take you home if you want," Conner offered.

"Okay, that would be great!" Hope agreed with a little flutter in her throat.

He grabbed her bag and put it in his trunk, and he opened the front door for her and drove to The Guesthouse.

He asked her lots of questions about camp and listened intently to her responses. Hope had never been in a relationship, but she felt really comfortable with Conner. She thought he would be a good guy to date this fall if he asked her out.

As he dropped her off, he asked, "Do you want to run Saturday morning at the track?"

"Sure!" Hope grinned, "See ya at school." She was still sweaty from the game and didn't want to give him a potentially smelly hug. She slipped out of the car, grabbed her bag when he opened the trunk, and hurried into the house with a smile and a wave. "Thanks for the ride!" she called to him.

He flashed her a thumbs up and drove away.

Judy Ann Koglin

CHAPTER EIGHT

Bible Study

Earlier this summer, shortly after Emma and Kendi had become Christians, they asked Aunty Nola if she could do a Bible study with them. Aunty Nola granted their request, of course, so they began studying the Gospel of John on Tuesday nights. Hope and Amie joined in when they were available.

Aunty Nola also taught the girls about the rest of the Bible in summary so they would get the big picture of creation, the fall of man, the early history of Israel, some prophesy and poetry, the life and crucifixion of Jesus, and the miraculous spread of the gospel through the early church. Aunty Nola was a born teacher, and the girls soaked up every word she said while they took notes in the notebooks that Aunty Nola had provided.

After a couple weeks, Emma asked Aunty Nola if they could do two sessions a week since they had such a short time before they had to go home, and they still had so much to learn. Aunty Nola loved that idea, and they agreed that the best time would be Sunday afternoons.

On one such Sunday, all four girls were home, and Nola was teaching from the book of Genesis about Jacob and his struggle to get permission to marry Rachel, the love of his life. The girls were shocked that Jacob's father in law Laban made Jacob work for him for seven years before he was allowed to marry Laban's daughter Rachel. They were then horrified to learn that Laban tricked Jacob and substituted her older sister Leah at the wedding and made Jacob agree to work another seven years to get to marry Rachel. It was a story that brought up a lot of emotion from the girls.

Kendi decided that maybe Jacob had this deception coming to him because earlier, he deceived his nearly-blind father to get the birthright blessing that was supposed to go to his brother Esau.

"Jacob really must have loved Rachel to be willing to work 14 years to get to marry her," Emma sighed.

"I've always wondered how Rachel and Leah could stand their dad after he used them as bargaining chips for Jacob's labor, with no regard to their wishes. I wonder if their relationship with their dad was pretty icy, or if they thought their father could do no wrong? And poor Leah, married to a guy who wanted to be with her beautiful younger sister…that must have been a lifetime of sadness for her, even if she did have lots of sons," Amie declared.

"I think the whole thing was terrible! I'm so glad that we live in the 21st century where women can make their own choices about if, when, and who we will marry," Hope declared.

"I agree!" Emma, Kendi, and Amie chorused.

"Amen!" Aunty Nola chimed in, and the girls giggled.

Aunty Nola pointed out that something good came out of all this because Jacob's twelve sons became the twelve tribes of Israel; so, a whole nation was born out of this man and his wives. The girls were excited to find out what happened next, so they jumped right into the upcoming chapters and learned that Jacob and his large family and abundant livestock were eventually able to leave Laban and went back to Canaan.

"Even though he wasn't thrilled to work for Laban," Aunty Nola said to them, "God blessed him, and he was able to accumulate great wealth."

The girls went on to read about Jacob's twelve sons, including Joseph with his coat of many colors and his dreams. Kendi and Emma were outraged that Joseph's brothers sold him into slavery in Egypt and lied to their father, telling him that he was killed by wild animals. The story got even more exciting when Joseph was thrown into prison after being falsely accused by his employer's wife.

"How much injustice is one person supposed to take?" Hope questioned.

"He did put up with a lot of abuse," Aunty Nola admitted. "However, Joseph never lost his faith in God and eventually became the second highest official in the whole kingdom. Shockingly, he even forgave his brothers later on down the line and helped them survive a famine. His story was a miraculous picture of how God uses everything for His good…you'll need to hear the rest!"

They read on to see what happened next. Amie read aloud the part about Joseph being let out of prison so he could interpret the pharaoh's dreams and was subsequently put in charge of the famine relief program that he pitched to the pharaoh.

Emma read the next part that talked about Jacob sending his sons to Egypt to buy grain. They didn't recognize Joseph, but Joseph recognized each one of his brothers and had a little fun with that before he eventually revealed the truth to them. Joseph loved and forgave his brothers and was in a position to be incredibly generous with them.

"Joseph's brothers were so cruel. I don't know if I could be so forgiving. It was really inspiring," Amie admitted.

"This is probably my favorite story in the Bible so far," Kendi stated with a satisfied smile.

"And we're just getting started," Emma responded, her dark eyes sparkling.

"We'll have to pick up with more lessons on Tuesday," Aunty Nola suggested. "Now, let's figure out what to make you girls for dinner."

"What about you?" Kendi asked.

"I'm going to eat with George…um, Mr. Femley, tonight and help him babysit his grandsons while his daughter is out with a friend."

"Oh, Taylor and Titus are cute!" Emma gushed.

"Aunty Nola don't worry about us, we'll figure out food. Hang out with your man," Amie giggled.

"Amie!" Aunty Nola retorted, shocked.

Judy Ann Koglin

CHAPTER NINE

Trouble at Stillwaters

Maybe it was the fact that it was August, and the girls were realizing that their great summer adventure was coming to a conclusion, or maybe it was just the call of the summer breezes off the beautiful lake, but each girl felt a little bit of magic in the air.

After Nola left to babysit with George Femley, the girls decided to splurge and go to Stillwaters, the fancy restaurant at The Lakeshore Resort. When they got there, they were greeted by the succulent scent of delicious hot food being prepared.

Once they were seated, Amie looked around the restaurant expectantly, hoping to see Josh. She was not disappointed.

When the busser came to fill their water glasses and announced, "Josh will be your server," Amie's heart skipped a beat. The girls gave her a look, and she tried to appear nonchalant.

"Ooooh, Jo-shhh," the girls teased.

"Shhh!" Amie shushed the others insistently.

The girls complied as Josh walked up, grinning. "How are The Guesthouse Girls tonight?"

"We're good!" they chorused.

"Well, our specials tonight include a freshly caught grilled salmon, with buttery dill and pesto, and our famous Crab Louie which is a spring mix of greens with tomatoes, cucumbers, eggs, slices of avocado, and, of course, crab meat, drizzled with thousand island dressing served with some freshly made toasted sourdough with whipped butter.

"Do the salads come in half sizes?" Kendi asked, indicating a smaller size with her hands.

Josh gave her a quick nod. "Yes, they do."

"Okay, I'll take a half Crab Louie and an iced tea," Kendi asked.

"Me too, but with a diet Coke please," Emma agreed.

"Me three, but with just water," Amie chimed in.

Josh turned and looked at Hope expectantly with his pen ready to write down her order.

"Uh, I'm going to look like a pig here, but I would like the salmon special, please," Hope requested, "and can I have some of the toasted sourdough bread as well? And a Sprite," she added.

"You got it!" Josh replied. "You won't regret it, Hope. People have been raving about the salmon all night."

Hope looked a little embarrassed, but Kendi reassured her with a quick shrug, "You're an athlete. You burn more calories every day before I even get up than I burn all day!"

The other girls agreed, and Hope felt better about her order.

The busser came back with an iced tea for Kendi, a diet Coke for Emma, and a Sprite for Hope. Josh followed closely behind him with special water for Amie that included a lemon slice and a sprig of mint with an umbrella from the bar.

"Oooo, an umbrella!" Amie gushed.

"Just for our most special customers," he told her with a wink.

Amie giggled. "Aww, thanks, Josh!" She hoped her face wasn't as red as she suspected it was.

Soon after that, the orders came out, and the girls dug in with gusto.

Hope declared that her salmon was one of the best meals she ever tasted, and the other girls loved their salads, wishing they had ordered them in full size.

Towards the end of the meal, Josh came out of the kitchen area looking shaken. He went to a couple tables and said something to them and then came to their table, his face drained of color. "Steve is going to finish up with you girls because I need to go."

"What's the matter, Josh?" Amie asked with concern.

"My mom had some sort of episode, and they are rushing her to the hospital in Wenatchee," he reported grimly.

"Can I go with you?" Amie asked compassionately.

"Really? Do you want to?" Josh asked. "I don't know when we can come home."

"Yes, I'm coming with you," Amie said firmly. "I'll figure out the rest later."

"Okay. Thanks, Amie. I could use the company."

"Kendi, can you pay for my meal, and I'll settle up with you later? Emma, when you see Aunty Nola, can you tell her what I am doing? I know she won't mind."

Kendi waved her hand, as if to tell Amie to get on the road with Josh and not worry about things. "No problem, Amie, just go!"

The girls shooed them out of the restaurant. They could see the two of them getting into Josh's car in the parking lot and driving straight toward the highway to Wenatchee.

"Yikes! We need to be praying for Josh's mom. Do you guys know anything about her health?" Emma asked.

"No," Kendi replied. "He seemed really scared, though."

"I'm glad Amie is going with him," said Hope. "She will be good for him. He *really* likes her."

The other girls nodded.

Just then, another waiter—Steve, according to Josh—came by and asked if they wanted coffee. They declined, and Kendi asked him to add Amie's salad to her bill.

Emma asked Steve about Josh's mom.

"Yeah, I think she has some health problems, but I'm not really sure what," Steve replied. He brought the girls their bills and processed their payments, thanking them for coming in.

The girls walked out of the restaurant toward the lake. "Do you want to go for a walk?" Kendi asked.

"Always!" Emma replied, and Hope nodded.

****

The girls walked on the sidewalk near the lake and talked about Hope, her new school, her upcoming move, and her experience at soccer camp.

"I am still really excited that I get to move here," Hope gushed. "I see no downside to it at this point. It looks like my mom will be able to come nearly every weekend this fall to train with the store's current owners, and she can stay at The Guesthouse with me. The store officially transitions ownership to my uncle sometime after Labor Day weekend. My mom will move up here in November, and both of us will move into the spare rooms at my uncle's house when his landlord moves to Florida.

"The soccer team is a bit of a mixed bag," she continued, shifting gears a bit. "The girls have been pretty nice. Some of them are great! I think it'll just be a matter of proving to the rest of them that I am not trying to be a threat to anyone; I just want to contribute to the team and get enough playing time that I might be noticed by colleges."

"Wow, things will really change for you. I'm jealous," Emma remarked.

"I get it. It feels like a Cinderella story to me. 'Poor single mom and her loner daughter get second chance at life due to a benevolent uncle,'" Hope commented ruefully.

"No!" Emma protested.

"How about, 'Standout athlete and her beautiful mother come to Chelan to share their talents to the community,'" Kendi suggested.

"Uh, Kendi's sounds much better," Emma voiced her opinion.

Hope sighed. "You're right. I need to change my attitude. Confidence is so elusive. Just when I start to get it, poof, it is gone!"

"I can relate," Emma confessed.

"Me too," Kendi agreed. "Do you girls want some ice cream?"

"Uh… always," Emma stated. Hope agreed, and they walked in the direction of the ice cream shop.

Judy Ann Koglin

CHAPTER TEN

Ice Cream Challenge

Kendi, Emma, and Hope walked over to the ice cream parlor and took a booth by a window.

"I hope people we know come by tonight," Emma commented.

"Well, it's Sunday night. A lot of high schoolers tend to stop by," Kendi replied.

A few minutes later, the doorbell gave a little ding, and a group of football players came in. Kendi and Hope recognized a few of them from a diner that they went to earlier in the summer. The guys were occupying booths a little bit away, but one of them, a tall brown-haired boy named Tanner caught Hope's eye and came over to talk for a minute.

"Hi, Hope! And, um…it starts with a K…"

"Kendi," she said, laughingly putting him out of his misery, "and this is Emma. Emma, this is Tanner."

"Hi, Tanner," Emma replied, noticing the cute little chin dimple he had when he smiled.

He nodded at her.

"Hey, did you girls hear about Josh's mom?" Tanner asked the group.

"Well, we know that she was on the way to the hospital, and Josh and Amie left Stillwaters to go there an hour ago," Kendi reported. "Do you know what happened?"

"She has cancer," he explained. "She was in remission, but a while ago, the cancer came back, and she has been fighting it. I think it is really bad right now."

"Oh, poor Josh!" the girls chorused.

"I'm glad Amie is with him," Tanner mentioned.

"Hey, girls, how's it going?" Tyson asked, joining the group. Tanner and Tyson were close friends and members of Chelan's football team. Tyson was medium height and had reddish-blond hair.

"We're discussing Josh's mom," Tanner told him.

"Oh yeah, that's sad." Tyson agreed, his smile disappearing. He scooted into the booth next to Hope. "Have you ordered yet?"

94

Tanner sat down next to Kendi. Emma scooted closer to the window to accommodate the extra person on their bench.

"Not yet," Hope replied. "I think I'm going to get a strawberry mango smoothie."

"I want a hot fudge sundae," Emma declared.

"What about you?" Tanner turned to Kendi.

Kendi pondered the menu. "Mmmm, I think I'll get a chocolate dipped cone."

"That sounds good. By the way, do you mind if we join you? We just kind of crowded in!" Tanner stated. "Tyson's girlfriend had to work tonight, and he was moping around, so I brought him here."

"You are welcome to join us!" Kendi replied with a laugh, and the other two girls nodded.

"If we get up to order, someone'll take our booth," Emma said. "I'll stay here while you order."

The other four went to the counter to place their orders. In the meantime, the bell on the door jingled signaled the arrival of more customers. To the girls' surprise, in walked tall blond Ben, flanked by Ryan with his amazing smile and chestnut brown hair and eyes, and their friend, lanky brown-haired Cody came into the ice cream shop and sat down with Emma.

"Hey girl, whatcha doing here all alone?" Ryan asked with a friendly smile.

Emma had a sharp intake of breath. Just a moment ago, she was feeling like a bit of a fifth wheel with her roommates and Tanner and Tyson. Now, she felt on top of the world sitting alone for the moment with three guy friends.

"Well, I'm not alone," Emma began. She was interrupted by Kendi and Hope's return.

"Are you guys going to order?" Hope asked.

"Yeah! We're going to do the monster sundae challenge," Cody reported.

"Really? Have you done it before?" Kendi asked.

"No, but my brother Joseph has, and he held the record for a while," Ben replied.

"No surprise given the amount of treats he eats at the bakeshop," Kendi commented with a laugh.

The monster sundae challenge, as written on a plaque near the menu, involved twelve different scoops of ice cream, five toppings, whipped cream, nuts, and a sliced banana. The whole thing cost $20. If one could finish the whole thing in seven minutes, they got a gift card for $20 for future purchases, and their picture and finish time went on the wall of fame. If they lost, they just had a pile of melty ice cream in front of them.

"Are you really doing it? All three of you?" Emma wondered aloud.

"I am!" Ryan stated.

"If he is, then I am," Ben agreed.

"If they do it, I'm doing it," Cody chimed in.

Ryan went up to the counter and told the servers that they wanted to do the challenge. The workers loved it when people attempted it, and the squeals of glee that erupted behind the cash register gave testimony to that fact.

The employees set up a folding table in the middle of the floor and put a row of three folding chairs behind it for the three participants. Emma took a photo with Cody's phone of the three guys standing behind their chairs. Cody posted Emma's photo on social media and encouraged his friends to come watch the monster sundae challenge. "Come on down!" read the caption. "Ryan, Ben, and I are doing the Monster Sundae challenge in about 15 minutes from now. Only the strong survive." The shop created a post about it on their page as well, hoping to draw in more customers.

The shift manager went over the official rules, including the fact that the whole sundae had to be consumed in seven minutes. No one else could eat their ice cream. They would get one scoop each of twelve random flavors between slices of banana.

The toppings were strawberry, chocolate, pineapple, blackberry, and marshmallow cream. Whipped topping was sprayed on top, along with chopped nuts and a bright red cherry.

Some of the football players shared Cody's social media post, and pretty soon, the place was packed with what seemed like half of Chelan's teenagers.

Kendi noticed that a young family who looked like they were coming for ice cream quickly turned around and went back to their car, presumably going to get their ice cream elsewhere. As the couple made their not-so-inconspicuous departure, Sierra arrived with her boyfriend Bryan. Hope waved to Sierra and Bryan when they entered.

The crowd circled the long table as the shift leader ceremoniously tied bibs around each of the boy's necks and handed them each a long-handled spoon and several napkins. The girls behind the counter brought out the three giant sundaes and set them before the contestants. The guy in charge started the stopwatch and the eating began.

Cody's strategy was to eat all the toppings first and then start with the ice cream once it wasn't so cold so as to prevent the dreaded brain freeze. Ben took bites that incorporated both ice cream and topping together, targeting the fruit flavors first.

Ben was methodically moving through the bowl, eating left to right at lightning speed.

People were taking photos from every angle, and the girls joined in the photography spree. There were many more girls who had showed up after seeing the social media posts, and they cheered the boys on.

At the halfway point, Ryan was getting close to the end, Ben was halfway through his bowl, and Cody had more than half of his ice cream left, although his toppings were gone. Ryan ate some more bites, then, with a grin, started stirring the remainder of the ice cream together to make an ice cream soup. Ben ate the remainder of the fruit toppings, leaving the marshmallow topping for last. His brother had warned him to avoid the marshmallow cream at all cost because the sticky substance took too long to consume. Cody was scraping the edges of his mound of ice cream so that it no longer resembled individual scoops of ice cream, just a grayish brown melted lump.

Ryan picked up his bowl of melted ice cream soup and drank it down with a whole minute left and let out a belch. Ben employed Ryan's strategy of making ice cream soup minus the lump of marshmallow cream piled up on one of the spoons. With 30 seconds left, he began to drink his soup.

At that point, Cody surveyed his mound of ice cream and was about to throw in the towel. Ryan jumped up and started massaging his friend's shoulders, coaching him through the process. Ben finished his ice cream and shoved the big spoonful of marshmallow cream into his mouth.

The crowd cheered for him and then started chanting "Co-dy, Co-dy," as the time ran out.

Unfortunately, Cody did not complete the challenge, but he made a good effort and vowed that he would be back to fight another time. Then, he staggered outside and threw up in the bushes.

Ben and Ryan were awarded their $20 gift cards. After the awards were given, the shift leader wrote the names "Ryan Sanders" and "Ben Brandon" along with their times on the hall of fame sign with a black marker and asked them for victory speeches. Ryan thanked the crowd for their support, asked everyone to delete the bad pictures they took of him, and said he was giving his gift certificate to Cody so he could return and fight for his honor. Ben said he was saving his gift certificate in case he ever had a date.

The crowd laughed at his self-deprecating comment and then dispersed. One of the football players grabbed Cody's bowl and downed the unattractive remains of his ice cream.

Ryan was feeling great, and Ben wasn't feeling too bad, so they asked the girls if they would like to take a walk with them. Kendi and Emma said yes, but Hope decided to stay behind with Sierra and some of the girls from the soccer team.

****

Emma, Kendi, Ryan, and Ben walked on the lake path. It was getting dark now, and the moon and stars shone bright over the lake.

Ryan and Kendi ended up in a conversation about some of their favorite bands and walked side by side on the lake path. Emma and Ben walked behind them, talking about her family's winery as they compared grape harvesting to apple and cherry harvesting and discussed the wine-making process.

"Don't they have a viticulture program at Washington State?" Ben asked.

"Actually, they have it at the branch campus in Tri-Cities where I live. Are you interested in the wine business? You could probably intern with my grandparents," Emma suggested.

"Actually, that does interest me," Ben admitted. "My parents and I will need to include WSU and the Tri-Cities on our world tour of colleges in a couple months."

"That would be good timing," Emma told him. "We will be either in the middle of harvest or working on wine. My little sister Riley loves to squish the grapes with her bare feet."

"That's fun! I'll have to join her," Ben agreed.

They overheard Kendi and Ryan discussing their favorite musicals, and Ben enthusiastically jumped into that conversation as they all tried to rank the top five musicals of all time.

Emma was tired and she sort of spaced out as she walked. Her thoughts turned to Connie Riley, a friend of Aunty Nola who had been attacked in her home by a burglar last month. Emma had formed a bond with her when they visited Connie in the hospital and Emma gave her a cuddly Teddy bear. Emma made a mental note to check with Aunty Nola about how Mrs. Riley was doing.

Speaking of hospitals, Emma couldn't believe that she had forgotten to check in with Amie about how Josh's mom was doing.

She sent a quick text: "Hey Amie. How is Josh's mom doing? How is Josh doing?"

She received a response from Amie momentarily.

"She has cancer," Amie's text read. "She had a high fever. They're running tests. They've brought down her fever a bit. It doesn't look great. Josh and his brother Rob and his dad are hanging in there.

They have strong faith. Josh and I are waiting in the waiting room because only two people can be back there."

Amie thought about what would be appropriate to say. She breathed a quick prayer to the Lord, as she had a few times since Josh and Amie left Stillwaters to hurry to the hospital.

Then, she texted back: "Josh's family is in our prayers. I'll let Aunty Nola know so she can pray."

Amie paused for a minute after receiving Emma's text, wondering why Emma hadn't already told Aunty Nola, but then remembered that Nola was with Mr. Femley tonight.

She chuckled softly at the thought of Aunty Nola being on some sort of a date, then typed: "Thanks for the prayers, Emma. I wonder if Aunty Nola and Mr. Femley are 'dating'?"

Emma's text reply came in with a ding: "I don't know, but it would be awesome if they were. They used to be classmates at Chelan High fifty years ago, and they are both so nice!"

"Hmmm… we'll have to figure that out later. Did I miss anything tonight?" Amie asked before tapping *send*.

"Yeah, check Facebook or Insta," said Emma's reply. "You'll see some boys we know who did the Monster Sundae Challenge."

"Okay, I'll look for it. This may be a long haul here at the hospital. I already told my aunt that Josh and I would not be in for work tomorrow."

"Okay! Let us know if you need us to do anything on this end. We got your back and Josh's."

Amie sent back one last text: "Thanks, friend."

Amie shut her phone case and told Josh about her conversation with Emma.

Josh replied, "We can probably head back when they get her stable. Then, you can go to work tomorrow, and I can take a shower and get some clothes and stuff for my dad and come back here."

"Okay, well, let's play it by ear for now," Amie responded resolutely. "I'm here as long as needed."

"Thanks, Amie. That is a lot to ask of you."

"I want to support you, and I'm glad you let me come with you."

"I really appreciate it. It has been an ordeal for our family for the last few years, especially my parents. My mom has felt miserable lately, and we were devastated to hear the cancer was back."

"We'll continue to pray. Emma's telling Aunty Nola, and I'm sure she will be mobilizing the whole church to pray…maybe even the whole town."

Josh smiled. "I have no doubt of that. She's always been good to my family. She used to bring us meals when my mom had cancer before."

Josh's dad texted him that his mom was medicated and sleeping peacefully, and he and Rob would be coming out to the waiting room soon.

Soon, they arrived and told Josh he could go in and see his mom for a few minutes. His dad said he would take him back to the room.

This left Amie with Josh's older brother Rob who bore a striking resemblance to his striking blond brother.

"So, I'm Amie," she said, extending her hand.

"It's nice to meet you," Rob replied as he shook her hand, "I'm Josh's brother, Rob. I actually live here in Wenatchee. I finished my degree in nursing, so this hospital is my stomping grounds. It is a whole different thing when the patient is your mom," he admitted.

"Oh, it must be awful," Amie responded with compassion.

"Say, are you Josh's girlfriend?" Rob asked.

Amie blushed. "No, just a friend. We work together at The Resort."

"Oh, I was just wondering. I haven't talked to him for a while, so I didn't know. He is a good guy, though. Just saying…"

Amie grinned. "He is a great guy. He'll probably meet his perfect match at U-dub this year."

"Maybe so," his brother considered. "He seems more like a WSU type of guy, but I guess he likes the UW engineering program better."

"That's what he said. I'm more of a Coug, myself," Amie revealed.

Rob fist bumped her. "I knew I liked you."

Just then, Josh and his dad emerged from the waiting room. Josh looked sad.

"They decided that they are going to admit her here at Wenatchee General," Josh's dad reported. "She may have to get transferred to Seattle, but she is stable now, and her doctor will examine her tomorrow and determine next steps. The doctors encouraged us to go home, get some rest, and come back tomorrow. I guess we should do that." Turning to Josh, he asked, "Do you want to follow me back to Chelan?"

"I guess that would work best. By the way, this is Amie. In all the craziness, I forgot to introduce you. Amie works with me at the resort."

The two shook hands. "Nice to meet you, Amie. I wish it was under better circumstances. Thanks for coming with Josh."

"My pleasure," Amie stated. "Glad to do it."

The four of them went back to their cars and said goodbyes. Amie climbed into the front seat of Josh's car, and they followed his dad back for the hour-long drive to Chelan.

On the way, Amie did her best to distract him with stories about the resort, her childhood, and The Guesthouse Girls. She got him laughing a few times and helped pass the minutes.

When they got home, it was close to one in the morning. He dropped Amie off at The Guesthouse and thanked her for coming with him.

"Get some rest," Amie admonished him. "I'm sure it will be another big day for you. If you need me for anything, don't hesitate to ask."

"Thanks again, Amie." He looked her in the eyes and said, "you are different than any other girl I know."

She blushed under the compliment, waved goodbye, and unlocked the door of The Guesthouse and went inside. She was happy that Josh had allowed her to accompany him to the hospital in Wenatchee tonight and was glad that he was willing to share how he was feeling with her.

She felt the weight of Josh's mom's illness and sympathized with the fear that Josh and his family was experiencing, but mixed in with that emotion was a little spark of hope that Josh might eventually end up being more than a friend.

CHAPTER ELEVEN

Life in the Laundry Room

The next morning, Amie went into work. Her coworkers were happy to have her because they had not been able to cover her shift in the housekeeping department and Maggie, who was going to be there, called in sick, and Samantha was on vacation.

Amie wore what she considered to be her grubbiest outfit: tan shorts and a stretchy white v-neck t-shirt, which was just a step plainer than all her other fabulous outfits. Amie couldn't help but accessorize a little, even if she was stuck down in the hot basement. She rolled a pink bandana and tied it into a headband and wore pink earrings.

She spent the day in the laundry room washing, drying, and folding hundreds of white towels and sheets, as they came in from the cleaning staff.

Every time she received a new bin of dirty linens, she stuffed them into the industrial-sized washing machines, measured the detergent and dumped it in, and got the machines going. Just when she had the machines tumbling, another cleaner would bring another full cart full of linens to be processed. It was hot down in the laundry room with all the industrial-sized washers and dryers running, and Amie couldn't imagine doing this every day.

It was redundant work, but it went by fairly quickly because she got into a rhythm. As soon as one of the wash machines finished a load, Amie found an empty dryer to transfer the wet linens, and when one of the dryers finished, she quickly unloaded it and started folding the items, just as she had been trained.

There were usually two experienced workers manning the laundry room on any given day instead of one inexperienced high school girl, but Amie was hustling to do the work of two. She didn't particularly like this laundry room duty, but it was part of the rotation of jobs she was doing at the Lakeshore Resort this summer.

The large Lakeshore Resort, first owned by her great grandpa and then by her grandpa, was now managed by her Uncle Bob and Aunt Debbie.

Amie's dad and mom had important roles at the resort that they were performing remotely from Montana, where they were taking care of Amie's grandpa this summer. Bob and Debbie wanted Amie to train in various areas of the resort so she could have a sense of what tasks all the different staff members had to perform. They told her this would be helpful to give her a good perspective in case she decided to become involved with the resort sometime in the future, even after college.

Amie's Aunt Debbie came down halfway through her shift. "Hi, Amie!" she called over the sound of the loud machines. "I'm so glad you were able to show up today. We would have been in bad shape otherwise. I think Bob would have had to run the laundry room, and that would have been a disaster!"

Amie smiled at the thought of Uncle Bob transferring wet laundry from the washing machines to the dryers, and she had to laugh. "I'm glad I could be here," Amie agreed.

"How is Josh's mom?" Aunt Debbie asked, concerned.

"I haven't heard from Josh yet today, but she was out of immediate danger last night."

"How are you enjoying laundry duty? It looks like you pretty much have it under control," she nodded appreciatively, looking around.

"It's going okay, but I decided that there is nothing like doing laundry all day to encourage me to do well in high school and go to college so I don't have to work in this hot laundry room as a career!" Amie laughed, then quickly added, "Although I will say that the ladies who normally work down here do seem to enjoy their jobs. They must be more used to the temperature down here."

"It is hot with all these machines going," Debbie agreed. "I think we should buy some large fans that Maggie and Samantha can use when they get hot."

"I think they would appreciate it," Amie replied. "Also, I think it would be helpful if we put some long shelves in here," she said, gesturing toward a space on one of the walls. "Then, we would have more areas for folded towels, and we could keep the sizes separate so things don't get mixed up."

"Oh, that's a great idea. I don't know why we hadn't done this before. That is why fresh eyes are so helpful," Debbie gushed. "If you have other good suggestions, please don't ever hesitate to tell me. We want to keep all our staff happy, as long as it doesn't bankrupt us!" she added with a smile.

"Okay," Amie replied, "I think we should put a water cooler down her so they can fill their water bottles with chilled, filtered water instead of the tap water that doesn't taste too great and never gets too cold."

Debbie typed something into her phone. A few minutes later, there was a ding from a returned text, and Debbie said, "Done. The guy who delivers water to the office upstairs will add a machine down here tomorrow."

Amie smiled. "I think Samantha and Maggie will be happy with the changes."

Amie and her Aunt Debbie worked side by side for the next hour folding towels. At one point, a cleaner brought in another bin of linens to be washed, and Amie deftly got the washers going.

"You *are* good at this. Maybe we should make you a weekend regular down here this fall," Debbie suggested.

Amie's face must not have hidden her disappointment because Debbie quickly said, "I was just kidding. I think we will offer you a front desk position on weekends. I think that is a better place for your skills."

"I would *love* that!" Amie gushed enthusiastically.

"Okay, it isn't final yet, and we still might want you to work in other areas sometimes, but we'll definitely get you up there some of the time. Brenda told me you did a fantastic job in that area. In fact, I received good reviews about you everywhere you worked. Hospitality must be in your blood," she laughed.

Amie laughed as well, followed by a big yawn. She realized how tired she was after her long evening in the waiting room followed by the drive back to Chelan from Wenatchee.

Amie's thoughts turned to Josh. He must be exhausted! She had really enjoyed spending time with him last night despite the scary circumstances of his mom's hospitalization. Amie had been praying for him and his family during today's long laundry shift, and she decided to send him a text to see how his mom was doing.

"Hey, Josh! Were you able to get any rest?" she texted.

His text read, "Yeah, I'm hangin' in"

"How's ur mom?"

"She's better, still going to Seattle tho. They are going to do surgery, and the doctors think they might be able to remove 100% of the new tumor."

"R u going 2 Seattle?"

"No, coming home 2nite. Mom insisted that I come home and get back to work, and dad and my brother agreed. I texted work so they know I'll b there. C ya tmrw!"

"K bye!"

Amie was happy for the optimistic news from Josh, and that put her in a joyful mood. She praised God for the good report and finished her shift cheerfully, knowing that she would probably catch a glimpse of Josh the next day.

Judy Ann Koglin

CHAPTER TWELVE

Talking with Tiffany

Emma had the day off from work, and she spent the morning lying in the sun at the park.

After sunbathing, she came home, took a shower, scrunched her perfect dark curls, and applied some light eyeshadow and mascara and a long-lasting red lip color that complimented her skin tone perfectly, followed by some matte gloss. She grabbed her tablet and walked to the resort where she was going to meet Ryan's mom Tiffany Sanders, owner of the Slip and Slide Water Park, for lunch at Beaches.

Tiffany was already seated at one of the square tables at the popular lunch counter when Emma arrived, and she beckoned Emma to come sit with her. Tiffany Sanders was an attractive woman that Emma guessed might be in her mid-to-late forties.

She had medium brown hair that fell in natural waves that she usually kept up in a ponytail. She wore tan shorts and a white and red polo shirt that had the Slip and Slide Water Park logo on the upper left just by her collarbone. She looked exactly the part of a busy water park owner.

Emma was glad she was taking time out of her busy schedule for the interview. Tiffany offered Emma a seat when she arrived, and she took it happily.

"I'm flattered you want to interview me for your blog," Tiffany started out. "Let's order, and then you can ask me questions." She handed a menu to Emma.

Emma decided to get a BLT, and Tiffany chose a half-Rueben sandwich and a side salad with thousand island dressing. Both of them ordered ice water with a lemon slice to drink. They flagged a waiter down who took their order to the kitchen and brought back their waters.

"Before we get started, I wanted to catch up and see how you are doing," Tiffany began. "It has been several weeks since you accepted Christ at the water park, and I went to your baptism. How have things been since then? Have you had a chance to learn more?"

"Oh, yes!" Emma replied enthusiastically. "Aunty Nola is taking us through a Bible study a couple times a week. We have learned so much about the Old Testament and the New Testament. She is such a good teacher!"

"Yes, I knew you would be in good hands with Nola," Tiffany responded. "I'm glad you are learning a lot."

"I really am. I'm really thankful for you for helping lead me to the Lord," Emma responded shyly.

"It was our pleasure. Every year, we invite a bunch of kids from church to the Slip and Slide for an after-hours party, but our purpose is that they bring friends who need to hear the good news about Jesus. The party is always a hit. It is so nice for kids not to have to stand in long lines."

"Yeah, it was really fun," Emma agreed.

The waiter returned with the sandwiches and Tiffany's salad. Emma's sandwich was the thickest BLT she had ever seen, and the toasted sourdough bread looked amazing. Tiffany's Rueben looked equally good with a large portion of beef stuffed into delicious-looking rye bread and a little thousand island dressing peeking out around the edges.

"Shall I pray?" Tiffany asked, and Emma nodded. Tiffany bowed her head. "Dear Lord, thank you for letting Emma and I have this special time together, and please help me communicate clearly. Thank you for this delicious food and the people who prepared it. We ask this in Jesus' name."

"Amen," said Emma.

"So, what is your first question?" Tiffany began, not wasting any of her or Emma's time.

Emma asked Tiffany to tell her about the history of the water park.

Tiffany shared the story of how the land was first acquired and what the first few attractions were. She talked about how she and her husband Pete–then a college professor–were able to acquire the park during an economic downturn. They worked hard, with Tiffany getting the park ready during the off seasons and both of them working there when school was out. They were even able to get some grants that helped them keep the place afloat. The park grew and became self-supporting and paid them a small salary. Since then, Pete had been promoted a few times at his college and now had a more lucrative position in administration, so they were able to reinvest most of the admissions revenue in the business to improve the waterpark.

Emma listened attentively while taking notes. When Tiffany fished, Emma asked some pointed questions about the business operations based on her online research of the water park industry.

Tiffany answered all Emma's questions openly. Emma really respected the passion that Tiffany had for the park, its employees, and the town of Chelan in general.

"How do you get people to go to the water park when you have a huge lake with swimming for free?" Emma asked.

"We do partnerships with hotels and run online package deals. We run social media ads. We have done some direct snail mail advertising on occasion. We put coupons in the Chelan ad magazines. We sell season passes to the locals. We've done a little bit of everything."

"Have you ever done any kind of promotions with Joe's Jet Skis?" Emma asked.

"No, I can't say that we have," Tiffany responded, "Why?"

"Well, my roommate Hope's uncle owns it, and he is buying the sporting goods store this fall. Maybe there will be some cross-promotional opportunities for next summer?" Emma suggested.

"Mmmmm … you've got me thinking. Let me know if you get a great suggestion in that arena," Tiffany requested.

"Will do," Emma replied as she munched on the last delicious bite of her BLT. After she finished her sandwich, she asked, "How is your employee turnover?"

"We have several people who come back summer after summer. Some are teenagers, and some are teachers who have the summer off. The teachers who work there mostly perform behind-the-scenes jobs because they don't want to confuse their young students, and they probably get enough interaction with little kids during the school year," Tiffany laughed. "We can usually staff the place with locals, so we don't usually hire summer staff from outside of the area."

"What was your biggest mistake and biggest lesson learned?"

"Oh, there were many. One lesson learned was not to do after dark parties. They seemed like a good idea at the time," Tiffany said with a wry smile that told Emma all she needed to know about the mix of teenagers and late events. "Now, when we do after-hours parties, we close the slides before it gets dark.

"Another lesson was to limit the number of things in the gift shop," she continued. "People aren't there to shop; they are there to pick up something they forgot, like sunscreen, goggles, beach towels, and so on. I was trying to make the gift shop into this smorgasbord of all things beachy, and we had a lot of inventory of swimsuits, jewelry, and even beach décor that never sold. That was a lot of money wasted just sitting on the shelf. It was a tough lesson. All the stuff was so cute, and I ended up selling it at cost to one of the retail shops in town and they had no problem selling it to their customers. Lesson learned: stay in my lane."

Emma took notes as fast as Tiffany talked. "What about concessions?" she asked. "What lessons did you learn there?"

"Well, concessions seem simple, but the stand is really a small restaurant, so we are subject to all the food safety rules that the Health Department demands of restaurants. They are good rules, don't get me wrong, but I had never worked in food service before, so they caught me by surprise. We got a good manager in there who runs a tight ship, so we don't ever get violations now. Also, with concessions, we limit the menu to things that we can freeze or have a long shelf life…except buns.

We buy buns from a local baker just as we need them, so they don't usually go bad. The menu includes hot dogs, slices of pizza, candy, soda, slushies, giant pretzels, and nachos. Most of our customers can find something they want off that menu. For those who are more health- or budget-conscious, they usually bring a cooler in their car and go outside and eat lunch and have their hand stamped so they can return."

Emma smiled. The waiter brought their ticket and refilled their water glasses. "Well, I managed to take up your whole lunch hour," she commented, looking at her phone. "Do you have anything else?"

"Nothing I can think of. I'll let you know if I get any inspiration. I still want to have you over for dinner sometime. We had mentioned it early in the summer when I first met you, then something came up."

"Oh, thank you, and thank you for lunch." Emma was hoping for a way to work Ryan into the conversation and finally thought of something: "One more question, if you don't mind? What role has your kids played throughout the years?"

Tiffany's face clouded for a brief moment, and then went back to her normal smile. "I guess that should be included in the 'lessons learned' section.

My daughter was around in the early days and she had to work side by side with us. She had her toys, and she just sat in the office for hours while we figured out everything. She later told us that she really resented being raised in the office of a water park. We really missed the mark. We thought she loved it there. She got to go on lots of water slides when no one else could, and she had her run of the park when she was a little older and a guaranteed paid summer job as a teenager. She didn't see it in the positive way we did, and she was angry with us for it. We've worked through some of these issues, but we could have handled things differently."

"What about Ryan?" Emma replied softly.

"Ryan is a totally different story. He has always loved everything about the waterpark: playing there, working there, all the business decisions, greeting the guests, all of it," Tiffany recounted, smiling. "He was born to work there, although I think he will choose a different field after college."

"Do you think he'll come back?" Emma asked.

"Not sure on that one. He loves it here, but there is a whole world out there, and he is kind of larger than life. Maybe he will meet someone at college who moves him away…who knows? Until then, I guess I'll get him every summer if I'm lucky."

"He's lucky to have parents like you guys. He speaks highly of you," Emma responded sincerely.

"Well, we are proud of him, too. He is a great son! By the way, where did the two of you meet? Emma?"

"We met the first weekend I was in town at the huge kickoff party at the lake that the church held."

"Oh yeah, I bet you met a lot of people then." Her text alert went off, and she looked down at the screen to read the notification. "Now I have to go since the receipt paper is jammed," she laughed.

"Thank you so much for lunch and the interview!" Emma replied.

"My pleasure! Let me know when I can read the interview. You have my number if you need anything!"

The two walked down the stairs to the parking lot and went their separate ways after a quick hug.

CHAPTER THIRTEEN

Daycare for Duke

After work, Ben and Kendi got in his car and went to Christopher and Lynsie's house to prepare for dog sitting. It looked like a well-maintained little cottage with a fresh coat of yellow paint and well-manicured lawn.

"What a cute house!" Kendi remarked.

"Yeah, it looks like they made some improvements and freshly painted it. It looks way better than before," Ben agreed.

Kendi walked up the porch steps and was about to knock on the front door that was painted bright blue with white trim to match the rest of the house, but Lynsie and Christopher saw them coming and stepped out onto the porch.

"Hi, guys!" Lynsie exclaimed. "You found us. Now, which house is yours Ben?"

He pointed out a much larger house a few doors down. "We've lived on this street my whole life," Ben revealed proudly. "I think they bought it when my mom was pregnant with my brother Joseph."

"We really like this street," said Christopher. "It is a nice established neighborhood with mature trees. It is hard to find a good entry-level house to buy in Chelan. We decided to buy one that was a little run down and do the improvements ourselves."

"I noticed the exterior paint. What else have you done?" Ben asked.

"We redid the flooring on the inside, painted the whole interior, replaced the trim, did a new facelift on the fireplace and had someone replace the countertops. Besides hiring him, we did everything else ourselves, " Christopher replied with pride.

"How did you know how to do remodeling?" Ben asked curiously.

"YouTube," Christopher admitted, "the great equalizer."

"It's the best," Ben agreed. "I gotta wonder who takes the time to post all those how-to videos. I've used them for my car repairs a couple of times. They saved my bacon."

"I know," Christopher chuckled. "There is a special place in Heaven for all those guys!"

Lynsie invited Ben and Kendi to come indoors, so she could show them some things about Duke. As she opened the front door, they were welcomed by a faint scent of cinnamon and vanilla.

Duke greeted them with a happy little bark.

Lynsie opened the pantry door and said, "This is where we keep Duke's food. It is best to feed him small amounts three or four times a day. He is little and doesn't eat much, but his breed tends to get low blood sugar, so they recommend that we feed him small meals throughout the day. We use this little bowl for his food and this one for water." Ben and Kendi nodded at the instructions and made mental notes while she pointed out each necessity.

"We take him outside for a potty break, of course. Just snap the leash onto his collar like this," Christopher demonstrated. "I'll show you where he likes to go." The three of them walked outside, and Christopher pointed out the shady area at the end of the road "He is really spoiled because we take him for walks a lot. If you have time and want to take him for a walk, I know he would really enjoy it. If you only have time to bring him outside for a short potty break, that is okay, too. I'll show you where we keep the scoop and the bags inside in case he decides to leave a present while you are walking."

Lynsie took up the conversation when the others came inside. "As for sleeping, Duke has a bed here which he sleeps in some of the time." She pointed at a soft, gray little dog bed that looked comfy. "However, he also likes to nestle in between us, so if you end up spending the night, you may have to share the bed with him. The bed in the spare bedroom is all made up with fresh linens if you decide to stay. Here is a key to our front door, Kendi." Lynsie handed her a key that was attached to a blue stretchy spiral loop that Kendi put around her wrist. "Do either of you have any questions?"

"What are Duke's favorite toys?" Ben asked.

Christopher showed Ben where they kept Duke's toys. "He likes to fetch and play tug of war."

"What if he gets sick or hurt?" Kendi asked. "Of course, I'm sure that won't happen."

"Duke goes to Lakeside Veterinary Services. They know him there. Hopefully, you won't have to call them, but if you do, here is their emergency contact info." Lynsie pointed to a business card stuck to the fridge with a yellow smiley-face magnet.

"That should be everything." Lynsie said with a smile. "We are just a phone call away if you have any questions. Feel free to text, too!"

"We'll do the morning feeding tomorrow, then if you guys can cover lunch, after work, night time tomorrow, all four feedings the next day, and probably just the first feeding the following day, that should be all." Christopher remarked. "We'll text you when we know when we plan to be back just to confirm."

"Sounds good," Kendi assured them. "Between Ben and I, we have it covered."

"We aren't worried at all," Lynsie stated as they walked Ben and Kendi to Ben's car.

"Have a great trip!" Ben and Kendi both called out the car window as they left. Kendi couldn't help thinking that this must be how it feels to have a boyfriend. She liked that feeling.

****

The next day, Kendi worked, but Ben did not.

Ben texted Kendi: "Do u want me to pick u up at noon and we can do the lunch feeding, or do u want me 2 just do it?"

"R u at home?"

"Yes, and u left the keys in my car last night, so I can get in."

"It would probably be easier 4 u 2 just do it, then u don't have to come to town to get me."

"Ok, I'll do this one and pick u up after work. I'm going 2 kayak with Cody after I take care of Duke, but I won't forget about u."

It was a slow day in the coffee shop, and Kendi was relieved when she was finally off work.

Ben showed up when Kendi was finishing her shift. He grabbed a hibiscus iced tea and drove Kendi to visit Duke.

Duke was happy to see the two of them and barked enthusiastically. Kendi poured the food and water into his little bowls which Duke consumed with gusto. Ben played with him a little while, then snapped the leash onto his collar.

"Shall we take him for a walk?" Ben asked.

"Sure," Kendi agreed.

Duke was panting with excitement to be taken on a walk, and he proudly marched ahead as if to show off the neighborhood to Kendi and Ben. They walked around the block and decided to discuss some of their favorite parts about the coffee shop.

"I like the brownies," Ben started.

"Well, I like the entertainment when we do open mics and concerts," Kendi countered.

"Oh yeah, me too. I was thinking more on the small scale."

"Okay…I like choosing the drink specials," Kendi stated.

"I like restocking supplies." Ben mentioned.

"Why?"

"Because it means that we have sold a lot of lattes and have made a lot of people happy, and we get to stay in business because we have customers," he smiled.

"Oh, good one. Speaking of customers, who are your favorites?"

"Well, I love our regulars; both the locals and the tourists who come in year after year when they are in town. I love their loyalty to us."

"I know! That is so cool," Kendi agreed.

"My favorite customers are the ones who get to know us as people. I love it when they remember our names, even if we aren't wearing our name tags," Ben shared.

"Yeah, that always makes me feel special."

"Who are your favorite customers?" Ben asked her.

"I love the people who come to Chelan from foreign countries. It is so cool that they have heard about us from that far away," Kendi revealed.

"I know, right? We are a small town in the middle of nowhere, but people from all over have heard of us."

"It does make me feel so fortunate to live here all summer. Not many people get that opportunity.

The lake is an easy walk from both work and The Guesthouse. I find myself there a lot swimming or lying in the sun and writing in my journal."

"How is that going? Are you still doing Bible study?"

"Yes! Aunty Nola is leading a Bible studies for us at home, and I am doing some reading on my own, too. The Bible is such a cool book. It's like a bunch of books in one. There are adventure stories, love stories, friendship stories, and lots more. I don't know why I never read it before."

"It can be pretty intimidating sometimes," Ben offered, "but it is helpful to break it up into individual stories. Then, you can focus on just that piece for a bit. If you think you need to read it cover to cover, you might feel tempted to read it as fast as you can and not really let it sink in. In my opinion, it is better to really learn the Bible than just to cruise through it really fast."

"That makes total sense. I like to read stories, but sometimes they are so good, and one leads to another that I end up reading for a long time."

"I think that is great because in that situation, you are engaged and paying attention. I think when you are just reading to check a box is when it can get less effective."

"Exactly, just like at school," Kendi grinned.

Duke, Kendi, and Ben finished their loop and ended up back at Christopher and Lynsie's house. Kendi unlocked the door, put Duke back in the house, and said goodbye to the adorable maltese.

Ben took Kendi back to The Guesthouse and asked her if she was planning to spend the night at Duke's or just come back.

"I think I will spend the night since Duke might want some company since his 'parents' are gone. I don't work tomorrow, so I can do the morning and lunchtime feedings, then I will walk back into town."

"That is a good idea. When do you want me to pick you up?"

"How about nine o'clock?"

"Sounds good," Ben agreed.

****

The next afternoon, Kendi walked back into town after she fed and walked Duke.

She had enjoyed spending the night at Christopher and Lynsie's house. When she slept in their guest bedroom, she had a dream about walking along a beach holding hands with Ben, laughing and looking really happy. She laughed to herself that she must be spending too much time with Ben if he had entered her dreams. However, she found herself thinking about it during the day.

I wonder if we will end up being a couple someday? she reflected.

She decided that it was pretty unlikely because she lived in Redmond and he lived in Chelan, and some other girl would probably snap him up. He was a good catch because he was good-looking, nice to everybody, a hard worker, and had a fun family.

Oh my, I think I am selling myself on the possibility of being his girlfriend. I'd better focus on his bad points. She grinned to herself. *Okay. Ben's bad points. Hmmm....well, he leads girls on because he is too friendly; he said it himself. What else? Can't think of anything beyond that right now, but I'm sure that is enough. Too friendly. Who am I kidding? That's not a bad point. Not really. That's it, I'm changing the subject!* She forced herself to think about what outfits she would wear the first week of school, the classes she would take, and how she'd organize her locker.

By the time Kendi reached the park, Ben was out of mind, and junior year consumed her thoughts.

She arrived at the beach park and spread her towel out by her favorite tree. She applied sunscreen, wiped off her hands on the towel, and pulled out her phone, and texted Bella, her best friend and neighbor from her house in Redmond.

Bella had not been super friendly this summer, but Kendi wasn't willing to give up her decade-long friendship, so she made an effort to text her at least twice a week. Kendi knew that Bella was hanging with partiers this summer and might have a boyfriend from that group, so she figured that was why she had rarely returned Kendi's texts.

When she didn't receive a text back from Bella, she decided to call her mom. Kendi and her mom Beth were close, and she missed their face-to-face talks. She last saw her mom in July when her parents came after the coffee shop was robbed. Her parents were really worried about her and offered to take her back home to Redmond, but Kendi had assured them that she was fine and the thief was in jail in Wenatchee, so they reluctantly left for their home in Redmond and let Kendi finish her summer. Her mom's phone went to voicemail, so Kendi left a cheerful message and then stretched out on her colorful beach towel, closed her eyes, and enjoyed the warm sun on her skin.

Kendi was startled when her phone rang about ten minutes into her tanning session. She looked down and saw that it was her mom. "Hey, Mom!" Kendi grinned as she answered the phone.

"Hi, Honey! I saw you called. Is everything alright?"

"Of course! I'm tanning on the beach in Lake Chelan in the summer with a light breeze. Things couldn't be more alright."

"I can imagine," her mom replied. "Remember, I spent a couple summers there when I was in high school."

"I know," said Kendi. "I can only imagine you selling those big black plastic vinyl records at the music store."

"If you must know, records were pretty much out at that time, but we did sell cassettes and these new things called CDs," Beth corrected her.

"I know, you told me before. I was just joking with you. But I wanted to tell you that I am dog sitting!"

"Really? Whose dog? Tell me about it."

Kendi told her mom the whole story about meeting Christopher and Lynsie, and she explained how she and Ben were job-sharing the dog-sitting duties.

Kendi's mom asked her to text a selfie of herself with Duke at the dinner time feeding, and Kendi agreed.

Kendi asked if anything was new in Redmond.

Beth replied, "Nothing new with us, but I think I saw Bella hanging out with some rough-looking kids at the mall the other day."

138

Kendi groaned inwardly…and outwardly. "Yeah, I don't think she is making great choices this summer, but I hope I'm wrong. She hardly ever replies to my texts these days. Maybe it will be different when I come home. Speaking of home, I'm excited to get my schedule. I know I will have zero-hour chorus and after-school jazz choir, so that will mean a lot of driving for you until I buy a car."

"I'd rather drive you both ways than for you to get a car right away," her mom told her. "I'd like for you to have your license for a while and get used to driving a few months before you get a car."

"Okay, but you'll probably get sick of driving me around."

"Are you kidding? You are growing up so fast– every time I drive you around is a privilege. As soon as you get a car, we won't see you again, as busy as you are!"

"Okay, well, I love our drives, too. You are a great mom. I guess I'll get going. I've got more relaxing to do," Kendi giggled.

"Sounds good," her mom agreed. "It won't be long until your summer is over. Enjoy every minute!"

"Will do!" Kendi responded and hung up.

She looked at the time and set her alarm to go off at 2:45. Ben was getting off work at three, and Kendi had arranged to meet him at the coffee shop, so they would both go to take Duke for a walk. Kendi happily dozed off, her long, reddish hair swept up in a messy bun.

When her alarm sounded, she gathered up her stuff in her tote bag and walked over to the coffee shop. She went inside and shyly took a seat until Ben finished his shift.

"Hi, young lady! Can I interest you in today's special, an iced chai?" her boss Mark asked her playfully.

"That sounds fabulous," she agreed.

"Ben is in the back room, and he will be right back so the two of you can feed Duke," Mark commented with mirth in his eyes.

Kendi grinned back. "What's so funny?"

"Oh, just that it takes two of you to dog sit a little eight-pound doggie," Mark replied.

"I know, it sounds silly, but they knew me already. Then, we found out that Ben lived so close, and it made sense that we share the love."

Mark raised his eye quizzically.

"I mean, share the job," Kendi stammered. She hoped that Mark interpreted her comment as love for the dog, not love for his good-looking son.

"I knew what you meant," Mark replied.

Ben walked in through the floppy kitchen door. "Ready?" he asked.

"Yep," Kendi replied, taking the deliciously-scented drink from Mark with a "thank you." Employees got one free drink per day, whether they were working that day or not.

Ben and Kendi drove straight to Duke's house and fed him. They took him for a walk around the same loop as the previous night, and Kendi had Ben take a selfie of the two of them with Duke. She sent the selfie to her mom and Lynsie and Christopher. Her mom said that they looked like a little family. Ben and Kendi both laughed at that. Lynsie replied to the picture with a smile and a dog emoji.

Ben asked Kendi if she was planning to spend the night at Christopher and Lynsie's again. After discussing it, they arranged that Ben would take Kendi back to the Guesthouse for dinner and then pick her up at nine. Kendi would spend the night with Duke again, and Ben would take her to work in the morning because they both worked at six.

****

In the morning, Kendi got up early to ensure that she had time to take care of Duke and shower.

When she got up, she threw her bedding in the washing machine first, took a shower, fed Duke, and took him out for a potty break.

By the time she came back in, she threw the bedding in the dryer on the quick dry setting and had played with Duke a few minutes and ate a breakfast bar.

Ben showed up at 5:45, just when the dryer was finishing its cycle, and played with Duke for a minute while Kendi neatly folded the linens and placed them on the guest bed. Ben then drove Kendi and himself to work.

Around eleven o' clock. Kendi received a text from Christopher that they would be home by noon, so Kendi didn't have to do the lunchtime feeding. She was busy with customers, so Kendi replied with just the thumbs up sign.

Around noon, Lynsie and Christopher pulled up and stopped in for a coffee. They handed Ben and Kendi each a blue envelope that felt like it contained a card. They asked how Duke was doing and if they had any trouble. Ben assured them that everything went smoothly, and they had a great time.

"Ben, we are going to need to get your cell number," said Christopher. "Since Kendi is leaving soon, we might need to ask for help again."

"No worries, man. I love Duke, he's the dog version of me," Ben joked as he added his contact info to Christopher's phone. "You can also knock on my door anytime."

"Thanks Ben. I bet you guys will miss Kendi around here," Lynsie commented.

"I don't even want to think about it," Ben murmured.

Kendi wondered if he was faking the sadness in his voice for Lynsie's benefit, or if he really was a little sad.

"Besides, no one else can do the cool lettering on the Drink of the Day sign the way she can!" Ben added with a smile.

They all laughed, and Ben and Kendi said goodbye to their friends.

Judy Ann Koglin

CHAPTER FOURTEEN

Last Week of Summer

Summer was rapidly winding down, and this Monday began the girls' last week before school.

Each of them was in for a busy week at their respective workplaces because Labor Day weekend started on Friday. That weekend symbolized the end of summer for the bulk of the tourists, and the weekend was projected to be even crazier than Memorial Day weekend was.

The Lakeshore Resort was hopping as usual, and Amie was acting as a rover this week, helping wherever she was needed most. Today, she was needed at the lunch counter, and she was happy to see that Josh was also working there, too. They were busy preparing for the rush and didn't have much time to talk until the lunch crowd died down.

145

When they had a moment, he filled her in on his mom's recovery and shared that she was back home and pretty much back to normal.

"Oh, I'm so glad. Cancer is so scary."

"Definitely," Josh agreed. "Oh, I forgot to tell you that the older couple who just finished lunch and went back to the pool had wanted to know if I was one of the Larson kids. I said, 'No, why?' and he said that I look like the rest of the family."

"Oh, Mr. Johnson is so funny," Amie laughed. "He comes this week every year and has known our family forever. He knows I am an only child. He was probably just making conversation."

"Well, when I told him we weren't related, his wife said, "Oh, good, then maybe you could date her."

"What?! Did she really say that?" Amie said with a red face that contrasted with her light blonde hair and blue eyes.

"Well, not exactly those words," he admitted, "that's just my translation."

"Did you tell her she was bananas?" Amie asked, partly embarrassed, but partly enjoying this conversation.

"No, I told her that was good advice, and I would let her know if anything happened."

Amie giggled nervously and remarked, "Well, I think the only thing that's happening right now is that I need to go back and help clean the kitchen."

Josh chuckled as she quickly ducked into the flapping doors of the kitchen area where she could reflect on that new development privately. As she cleaned up the kitchen that afternoon and did some prep work for the dining room for the nightly rush, she found herself smiling from time to time as she pondered what Josh had told her.

****

Meanwhile, at the General Store, the staff members were preparing for their end-of-summer clearance sale. Emma's job today was to help organize a bunch of summer merchandise that would be marked down and make some 40% off signs to put on the summer racks on Wednesday.

Tricia explained, "This sale will help reduce the summer inventory. After this week's crowds purchase a lot of the stuff at 40% off, we might go back and mark everything down again and sell the remaining stuff to late-season tourists."

Emma loved sales. She'd had her eye on some swimwear and was thrilled to find out that it was about to be marked down. She asked Tricia if the employees were able to buy things, too.

"Oh, yes," Tricia replied. "I always stock up as soon as we get the codes updated in the register. I should have that done by two this afternoon. I'll let you know so you can shop today or tomorrow before the sale starts on Wednesday. What are you gonna get?"

"I'd like to buy a couple swimsuits and cover-ups. I also want to get something for Aunty Nola, because she has been so wonderful to all of us this summer. I think I might get something for Taylor and Titus, Kim's little boys, too."

"Those little guys are so cute! I bet they give Mr. Femley a run for his money, though."

"Probably so!" Emma laughed.

****

Over at Brandon's Coffee, the shop was crowded with visitors, and staff members were getting prepared for another weekend concert event while staying busy serving pastries and preparing lots of iced coffee drinks for their morning guests. Many of the visitors who stayed in Chelan this week were regulars who came the same week every year and were familiar with the local businesses and even knew a lot of the owners. Rachel and Mark Brandon met several such customers on Monday.

They were happy to see so many familiar faces come back and enjoy their shop.

Ben had told Reed and Kendi in advance that this was always the best week for tips because the last week of summer crowd tended to be very generous. Kendi was hoping this would be true since the goal she set before coming to Chelan was to end the summer with $2500, and she was currently just short of this amount, especially since she kept spending this summer. She reflected on her shopping spree in Wenatchee over the Fourth of July weekend, the ice creams the girls would buy on their evening walks, and the occasional lunches and dinners out with her roommates.

All worth it! she decided.

****

Hope was enjoying a beautiful day checking out watercraft to visitors. The blue colors of both the sky and the lake were deep and vibrant, and the nearby grass looked especially vivid-green.

There was a slight breeze to keep things from getting too hot, and there were a couple birds flying overhead. Hope reflected on the beauty for a moment and was overwhelmed with gratitude that this charming town would be her new home.

She turned her attention back to her job and got busy assembling the paperwork for the ten o'clock jet ski renters who were scheduled to show up around 9:45. She looked up to find an attractive couple waiting patiently for her to notice them.

"How can I help you?" Hope asked politely, but then smiled when she recognized the male customer and added in a friendly voice, "Oh, hi, Conner! Are you here to rent equipment?"

"We are," he said, grinning. "I haven't seen you for a while."

She looked down, scrutinizing the reservation list with a frown, "I don't see your name on our reservation list." Hope wondered silently who the pretty brunette with him was.

"It's probably under Sarah," Conner realized.

"Oh, yes...I see it here...Sarah Johnson, correct?" Hope confirmed.

"That's me," the girl smiled brightly. "We rented a two-person Jet Ski," she said, looking at Conner.

Hope pulled out a waiver with a clipboard and pen. "Okay, here's your paperwork to fill out."

While Sarah filled out her waiver, Hope turned to Conner. She was surprised how deflated she felt. She was initially so excited to reconnect with him, but seeing him with Sarah, whoever she was, made her not so enthusiastic.

150

"How's it going, Hope?" he asked.

"Pretty good," she replied evenly.

Sarah asked, "Are you here for the summer?"

"I was, but now I'm staying in town and going to Chelan High," Hope responded.

Sarah's face lit up like a Christmas tree. "I'm so excited about that, Hope! You look like a runner. Are you going to run cross-country and track?"

Hope answered, "Not cross-country, but soccer, basketball, and track." she said flatly. "I've started doing practices, and I went to soccer camp."

"That's so great," Conner said approvingly. "Sarah is on the soccer team and track team, too."

"That's right," Sarah said. "I've been gone all summer, but I heard we were getting a new player. It is nice to meet you, Hope."

Hope nodded politely and tried to force a smile.

Hope showed them where to grab life jackets. They left with one of the other staff members to get their Jet Ski, and Hope felt a twinge of envy watching them laugh as they took off together.

Stop that, Hope, she thought to herself. *Of course he had a girlfriend. I was stupid to think that he liked me. He must have been distracting himself until she came back to town. I'm too busy for a boyfriend anyway*, she reminded herself as several more customers approached the shack for their rentals.

An hour later, when Conner and Sarah returned from their ride, Hope was busy, but they caught her eye through the shack's open door and waved.

"See you tomorrow at practice!" Sarah called.

Hope flashed her peace sign, then returned her attention to the customers she was working with.

The rest of the day passed quickly as she and the rest of the staff smoothly handled all the reservations. Hope had morning practice from nine to noon the rest of the week, and she reminded Joe of that as she was leaving for the day.

"I remember," he said. "So you will work after practice until closing the rest of the week, right?"

"Right," Hope confirmed, "and I'm looking forward to shifts next door after school starts."

"We'll see how that goes, Hope. You'll be in a new school, and you have your new team, so you'll be busy. I'd love to have you at the store, but your school and sports are the priority right now."

"I know," Hope said dejectedly. "I want to work at least a little bit."

"Don't worry; we'll get you in, but you still need to be a kid. Your mom didn't get that opportunity, so we both want to make sure that you have the whole high school experience. I could not be happier that all three of us will be together, and we will be a real family."

"I'm happy about that, too, Uncle Joe." Hope realized she was a fortunate girl to have an uncle who cared about her and her mom so much. "I guess I'll head out now," she said tentatively.

"Go," he agreed. "We'll see you tomorrow."

Hope walked back to The Guesthouse with the spring in her step restored. She was so happy that she was going to get to live in Chelan and couldn't wait until November when her mom Megan would be here full-time, too. If things didn't work out with Conner, so be it.

She was living in this beautiful town, and that was enough for her.

Judy Ann Koglin

CHAPTER FIFTEEN

Drive-In Dates

The next day, Kendi was working the earliest shift at Brandon's, filling to-go boxes with donuts and pastry orders as well as backing up the espresso counter when they had rushes of customers. She was really glad she had ended up working here. She had spent a lot of time with the various members of the Brandon family this summer and had gotten to know Reed, the other summer helper, too.

Even now, she didn't know how she and Ben felt about each other, but she decided that they were probably just friends. His flirtatious vibe was probably just friendliness, and she was perfectly fine to just be part of his tribe.

As she was carefully adding the last maple bar to a box of a dozen mixed donuts, she looked up to see Ryan in front of her.

"Hi, beautiful!" he said with his signature grin.

She blushed. "Hi, Ryan! Are you looking for Ben? I think he's getting lids in the back."

"No, I actually was looking for you. I haven't seen you in a while, and I was wondering if you might want to go to the drive-in theater? They are showing Tom Hanks movies this week, and I think tonight's movie is 'Forrest Gump.'"

"By ourselves?" Kendi asked.

"No, there are tons of cars there," he laughed. He understood her meaning and said, "Well, I was thinking by ourselves, but it would be fun to bring friends, too. Maybe Ben would want to come?"

"Come to what?" Ben asked returning with a couple sleeves of lids.

"Kendi and I were talking about going to the drive-in tonight. Buy one, get one free popcorn on Tuesdays," he said with a wink. "Do you want to come with us?

"Oh yeah, I love being the third wheel," Ben said dryly.

"We could bring one of my roommates, too," Kendi said.

"That sounds fun! do you know if any of them are free tonight?"

"I assume so, because it doesn't start until later at night, right?" Kendi asked.

"I'll text Emma and see if she can come," Ben decided, typing into his phone.

Before he pressed "send," Emma walked in the door. "It looks like this is the place to be!" Emma said cheerfully.

"I was just texting you!" Ben exclaimed, pushing "send" on his phone.

"What are you doing here?" Kendi asked her friend.

"Well, I was just coming over for a raspberry iced tea, and Tricia asked if I knew some tall guys who could hang a Summer Clearance Sale banner on our building Wednesday morning. Ben, I was going to ask if you and your dad could do it, but now that I see Ryan, maybe you and Ben could do it?" she questioned in a sweet voice.

"Well, when you ask like that, how can we refuse?" Ryan responded. "But it will have to be early, like at six in the morning. Will that work for you, Ben?"

Ben groaned. "That is my day to sleep in, but okay, I'll do it."

157

Emma looked down at her phone and read her text from Ben. "Oh, by the way, yes on the drive-in tonight. Sounds fun!"

"Okay, we'll pick you up at eight at The Guesthouse."

"Sounds good!" the girls agreed.

With that, Ryan and Emma both left to go back to work, and Kendi and Ben got back to their tasks.

****

When two in the afternoon came, Kendi said goodbye to the remaining staff and went home to change into her swimsuit to lay out in the sun by the lake. When she got there, Amie had also returned after an early shift, and the girls walked to their favorite tanning area.

While they basked in the late summer sun with the nice breeze, they talked about their summers.

"Have you seen Josh lately?" Kendi asked.

"I did today," Amie replied and told her about the weird exchange they had that morning.

"It sounds like he likes you, or he would not have told you about what that old couple had said," Kendi offered.

"That's kind of what I was thinking, but I don't want to read too much into it." Amie explained.

"He might've just been laughing at it with me. The speculation is driving me crazy."

"Maybe it's time to get out and do something fun," Kendi suggested. "Me and Emma are." She told Amie about "Forrest Gump" playing tonight at the drive-in and about the arrangements they had made with Ryan and Ben earlier in the day.

"That's funny," Amie commented, "one of the dishwashers was mentioning the drive in today at work. It's half-price popcorn night. She was trying to get a group together to go. Maybe I'll text her." She picked up her phone and exchanged a few texts with the dishwasher, then laid back and closed her eyes and relaxed as the sun warmed her tan skin.

She was startled by the sound on her phone alerting her to a new text. She read it, then turned to Kendi and said, "You will not believe what happened. I texted the dishwasher Maria about the movie, and she said that her car was full, but she thought that there were going to be two cars of our staff. She said to hang on a minute, and someone would text me back. Well, guess who just texted me back? JOSH!" she shrieked without waiting for a reply from Kendi.

"What did he say?!" Kendi asked excitedly.

Amie read the text to Kendi: "It looks like Maria's car is too full for the drive-in tonight, and we are the odd men out, so I was wondering if you would like to go with me in the reject car?" Amie laughed when she read it.

"Well?! What are you going to say?" Kendi asked.

She asked Kendi for her opinion: "How about this? 'I would love to be a reject with you tonight.'"

"Perfect." Kendi replied. "It is lighthearted but accomplishes your objective. That's what you want right? To spend some time with Josh outside of work to see if this might be a thing? Besides, we will be nearby to chaperone and so will the carload from your work."

"Yes, I guess you are right," Amie said, laughing at the chaperone comment, "and I will be there to chaperone you and Emma!"

****

That evening, the three girls had a light dinner and got ready for the drive-in. Aunty Nola had insisted that each of the girls get permission from their parents. Once texts were sent and permission was granted, the girls tried on about six outfits each before they each settled on "The Perfect Outfit."

160

Kendi wore white capris and a green v-neck short-sleeved sweater that matched her eyes. She wore them with white strappy sandals that had a little heel. Emma wore a black short skirt with a frayed hem and a fuchsia stretchy shirt with a lace overlay. Her sandals were black flats. She wore a fuchsia headband around her dark curls, and the other girls assured her that she looked really pretty.

Once they were all satisfied with their hair and makeup, they came down, and Hope and Aunty Nola pronounced them beautiful.

Soon, Ryan and Ben pulled up in Ryan's dad's convertible, and the boys came to the door to pick up Emma and Kendi.

Shortly after that, Josh showed up in his car and knocked on the door to get Amie. She wore a light blue denim skirt with a pink t-shirt and a matching denim vest. She wore pink flat sandals, a pink bracelet, and her bob was gathered in a scrunchie.

"You look like Sandy from Grease!" Josh blurted.

"That was my inspiration for this look," Amie said, laughing. "I'm glad you noticed, Danny."

Josh laughed too.

"Well, let's go Sandy!" he joked as he held the door for her.

"Have fun!" Hope and Nola called after them.

161

****

Meanwhile, Ryan, Kendi, Ben, and Emma were having a great time at the movies. They enjoyed popcorn and sodas, and the boys shared stories of their antics growing up in Chelan. The four of them had to keep shushing each other during parts of the movie that they had particularly wanted to see, but other than that, it was a great experience.

After the movie, they drove to the park and sat at a picnic table.

Ryan asked Kendi if she was glad to be going back home on Monday.

"Yeah, I had the best summer ever, but I miss my family and my friend Bella, although we haven't talked much. She was going to come visit this summer but decided not to come," Kendi said sadly. "I am looking forward to the music program at my school, though. It'll be fun to be an upperclassman. We get lockers upstairs this year."

"Your school has an upstairs?" Ben laughed. "Chelan is so small; we barely have a downstairs."

"He's just kidding," Ryan shot back. "How 'bout you, Emma? Are you looking forward to home?"

"Not really," she admitted. "I miss my family, but Chelan has been so magical, and Pasco doesn't have the same vibe, at least, not for me. I've found good friends here but things are different at home.

162

A lot of the kids I know from my neighborhood are doing drugs or have been in trouble with the police. I've a hard time finding good friends.

"Emma, make sure you find a good church to attend and see if you have a Young Life group at your school. You said you go to a huge school, so there are probably a lot of other Christians there that you haven't met yet," Ben encouraged.

"I hope you're right…but I am really going to miss you guys and all the fun we had this summer," Emma said, looking at Kendi. The girls giggled as they continued to recall some of their summer fun.

"Well, I assume you girls will get your driver's licenses when you get back home, so maybe you can drive up here and visit some weekend," said Ryan.

"Hope wants us all to come and snowboard together, so we are going to try to plan something. I doubt my parents will let me drive that far by myself, but I will figure something out," Emma assured them.

Kendi agreed that her parents definitely would not let her drive all the way to Chelan alone, but she said they would probably want to come anyway, so it wouldn't be a problem to get there.

"We probably need to be getting home," Kendi said, glancing at the time on her phone.

"Ok, yeah, I don't want you to turn into pumpkins," Ryan teased.

"Whatever," Emma responded playfully. "You would just need to bring the glass flip-flop to see which girl it would fit!" The four laughed together at that.

They got in the car, and the boys walked them to the front porch and said goodnight. It was a little awkward, and there were no kisses goodnight or even a hug or handshake. That was perfectly fine with the girls, though, because it would have been weird in a group, and they felt that the whole night had seemed a little off.

When they went inside, Amie had already arrived home and had told Hope and Aunty Nola about her night, so she recapped the whole evening for Kendi and Emma. It had gone really well, and they had spent a lot of time talking about everything from school, colleges, the resort, church, and more. Amie decided that she really liked Josh and was hoping they would get to go on an official date at some point. She shared that he gave her a hug at the front door, and she thought it was really sweet.

The girls were happy for her and assured her that she and Josh would be a perfect couple if they decided to start dating.

Emma reported on their night: "Well, it was pretty much like hanging out with a brother and his friend. No romance at all. Completely platonic…probably because we are leaving so soon, or maybe they weren't that into us. It was like a group of friends going to the movies."

"That's because that's what we are," Kendi reminded her.

"I know, but I was still hoping to meet someone special this summer," she said wistfully.

"You are so funny, Emma," Hope laughed. "I think you dodged a bullet. I know I'm in no rush to date." Hope sated emphatically.

"I thought you would end up with Brett or Conner," Amie said seriously. "Maybe you still will."

"Brett has already left for college and Conner has a girlfriend, so I think that ship has sailed," Hope revealed.

"I didn't know Conner had a girlfriend. What is her name?" Amie asked.

"Sarah. She is on the soccer team."

Amie laughed. "Sarah is not his girlfriend. She's his cousin! Her family has been traveling in Europe this summer, and they just got back."

"Really?" Hope said not able to hold back a smile, even though she tried to be nonchalant.

"Pinky swear. You will love her!" Amie confirmed.

"Maybe the ship hasn't left dock, after all," Aunty Nola commented, continuing the boating analogy.

"Hmmm… I still think I'll steer clear," Hope responded. In an effort to avoid the subject, she announced, "It's late. I'm heading to bed." The others agreed.

****

When the girls got upstairs and out of earshot of Aunty Nola, Emma gathered the other girls together in her room for a quiet conversation.

"I want to give Aunty Nola a big gift, and I was wondering if all of you could afford to go in with me and have it be from all of us?"

"Of course!" Kendi and Amie quickly replied.

"What did you have in mind?" Hope asked.

"Well, I was thinking that we could get her a new grill for barbecue since she always likes to host gatherings, and her grill is on its last legs.

Based on my online searches, and we could get a good one from a hardware store in Wenatchee. The one I liked is normally $399, but it's on an end-of-season closeout for only $229 plus tax. I think we could have one of our parents pick it up on their way through town if anyone has room in their vehicle."

"Mark Brandon has a truck, and he goes into town on the regular," Kendi replied. "I know he would pick it up for us and sneak it into the backyard."

Hope stepped out of the room while Kendi was talking. When she came back, she handed Emma $65 cash. "This is my share," she said with a smile.

The other two girls quickly went to their rooms and brought back their contributions. Emma turned the money over to Kendi along with her own $65.

"Please see if Mr. Brandon can do it," Amie implored, "and if he does it, please let me know when he puts it behind the house because I can make a huge green bow for it."

The other girls giggled at her.

"What?"

"How do you know how to make bows?" Emma asked.

"I watch tutorials on YouTube, and I love Pinterest," Amie admitted. "Why are you laughing?"

"Because you are naturally good at everything and if you don't know something, you learn it from a video," Emma replied. "We aren't laughing *at* you; we are just lucky you are our roommate because you have so many talents."

"So do all of you!" Amie protested.

"We are a good group. We all can help each other when we can," Kendi agreed.

"I'm going to miss you girls!" Amie cried.

"Let's try to have group texts at least once a month," Hope suggested.

"Great idea," the other girls agreed before dispersing to their rooms.

CHAPTER SIXTEEN

The Last Saturday

It had taken some work, but Mr. Femley had agreed earlier this summer to allow Emma to plan a party to celebrate the store's 80th anniversary.

It wasn't going to be as big of a shindig as Emma had hoped, but they were going to thoroughly decorate the store with streamers and balloons. There was signage on the reader board, a huge sheet cake in the back by the ice cream counter to be cut at three o'clock, and a sidewalk sale outside. The local radio station had agreed to do a live broadcast around noon and provide some giveaways.

The best part of all, in Emma's opinion, was that Mr. Femley's somewhat-estranged son, Robert, was coming from Seattle to celebrate, along with his wife Christina and teen sons Dustin and Jordan.

Reuniting Mr. Femley and his son was the real reason Emma wanted to plan this event in the first place. It had taken some urging, both on Emma's part and later from Robert's sister Kim, to get him to attend, but he eventually agreed to come. He enjoyed boating, so he was going to bring his boat and stay in his camper.

Emma organized the party with help from Tricia and Ashley and advice from Kim. Mr. Femley signed off on which activities they could include, but he let the girls plan the details. They had shooed Mr. Femley out the previous evening and went into full-on decorating mode. Rachel Brandon provided the sheet cake, and Tricia determined which items to include in the sidewalk sale. The event was going to run all day, but the major festivities would be at noon. Tricia agreed to run the sidewalk sale outside and rigged up a cash register station for those sales. Ashley would cut the cake and serve it to guests. Ellen would occupy her regular place at a checkout register backed up by Emma, and throughout the day, they would rotate to accommodate lunches. Mr. Femley would be freed up to mingle with guests who wanted to come by and congratulate him, and Kim would be off work so she could hang out with her brother, his wife, and their kids.

Before they knew it, Saturday had arrived, and Emma and her little crew were putting the final touches on the decorations before the store opened at eight o'clock in the morning.

At 7:45, Mr. Femley arrived at the store with his daughter Kim, his son Robert, and his daughter-in-law Christina.

Robert and Christina looked like they stepped off the pages of a yachting magazine with their designer clothing and perfect hair. They were the owners and operators of a marine sales and repair business that catered to the tech millionaires in the Seattle and Bellevue areas. They had inherited the business from Christina's dad when he had passed away unexpectedly several years ago. Mr. Femley gathered the staff around to introduce them to Robert and his family.

"Oh, so you're Emma!" Robert smiled as he shook her hand. "I've got to say, you're pretty persuasive. Have you ever thought of going into sales?"

Emma laughed, recalling their conversation over the phone last month where she tried to convince him to come to Chelan to celebrate the store's anniversary. "You never know," she countered. "I'm just glad you're here. But where are your kids?"

171

As if on cue, Dustin and Jordan walked through the doors with their cousins Taylor and Titus on their shoulders. The little boys were having a grand time hanging out with the big boys. Dustin and Jordan both looked like their dad with tanned faces, perfect hair, and designer resort clothing.

Way out of my league, Emma thought with a sigh.

She had no time to focus on that, though, because the store was about ready to open.

Right before eight o'clock, Emma was surprised to see Aunty Nola show up.

Aunty Nola greeted Kim, then threw her arms around Robert in a huge hug. "Robert, it is *so great to see you!*" she said the words slowly and emphatically. "It has been *years!*"

"Hi, Mrs. Milton," he greeted her with a huge grin and returned her hug. "I guess we were just busy with the business and the kids' sports."

"Well, you're here now to celebrate your dad, and that's what matters!" Aunty Nola assured him. She greeted Christiana warmly and then turned to the boys. "Dustin and Jordan, I know you don't remember me, but I remember you when you were little, like Taylor and Titus. It's so nice to see you!"

"Thanks, Mrs. Milton," the boys both said, embarrassed by her attention.

Ellen and Tricia greeted Mr. Femley's family and Ashley whispered to Emma, "hashtag eye-candy," nodding to the boys. Emma giggled and agreed.

Mr. Femley turned the red and black sign around on its chain so the side that faced out to the sidewalk said, "We're Open, Come on in!" and the side facing the inside of the store said, "Sorry, We're Closed," and had the store hours listed.

The whole day was special, and Emma witnessed dozens of locals coming in to congratulate Mr. Femley, and some brought cards. Ellen had the foresight to invite the vendors to the celebration so several of the sales reps who supplied the stores came with gifts and some had sent flowers in advance. Emma's roommates stopped by at different times, when they had a chance, so they could witness the fun and put their names in the drawings that the radio station was doing.

At six o'clock, Mr. Femley told them that the family would finish the day and close up the store. Emma and Ashley were glad to go so they could get ready for the coffee shop tonight. They hugged and congratulated themselves for putting on a fun event for Mr. Femley and his family to enjoy and celebrate the longevity of Femley's General Store, and they dispersed from the parking lot.

****

Before Amie knew it, Saturday had arrived, and it was the last coffeehouse concert of the season.

Kendi and Emma's parents would be taking them home tomorrow afternoon. The Olsen family would be moving out of Amie's house, and she and her parents would be able to move back in on Tuesday, the first day of school. The Guesthouse Girls would be going their separate ways…at least, for now.

That night at the coffee shop, the concert portion of the evening had gone smoothly. Joseph and the rest of his band had outdone themselves, playing to a packed house. It seemed like half the town had shown up, even the older people like Aunty Nola. Mr. Femley even made an appearance with his son and older grandsons. It was fun to see Aunty Nola hanging out with her friends. Hope's uncle Joe also made a rare appearance, sitting with the couple that he was buying the sporting goods store from.

By ten o'clock, many of the older crowd left, and the open mic session began. Mr. Femley and his family and some of Emma's coworkers from the general store stayed late, as well as Aunty Nola. Amie's aunt and uncle, who managed the resort, were also in attendance, as were her parents who had arrived back in town earlier than expected.

They were going to stay in a trailer on their property until Tuesday when they could move back into their home.

The reason so many people they knew stayed late tonight was that The Guesthouse Girls were going to sing a song together. The girls had told their co-workers, but they didn't expect so many to show.

It had taken some pleading from Kendi to convince the other girls to perform, especially Hope, but she eventually won them over. They had spent several hours this week practicing and they were ready to give it a go. Their names were announced, they stepped up to the stage, and Joseph handed each of them a mic.

Kendi bravely said a few words: "We are The Guesthouse Girls! We started out as strangers, but we became like sisters this summer. We want to give a shoutout to Aunty Nola, for allowing us to live at The Guesthouse this summer. It was an amazing experience for all of us. We also want to thank our employers for taking us on this summer. We all learned a lot. Chelan is a special town, and we were fortunate to be here these past few months. We wanted to find a perfect song and we dug *deep* to find this one. It is from the 80's…it's "Friends" by Michael W. Smith!"

Kendi took her place behind the keyboard and started to sing the first verse to the song, which was familiar to a lot of the adults in the room. The verse talked about how a chapter in the lives of friends might end, but they will remain close.

When she had finished the verse, the other three girls joined her on the chorus, at first nervously, then gaining confidence when they realized that many in the crowd were singing along with them.

Hope was initially the most reluctant one to participate, but she surprised herself once they started singing and thought, *This is the coolest feeling, as long as no one actually hears my voice!*

Kendi continued to sing the verses, and the crowd joined in by singing the chorus with them.

The girls had tears in their eyes as they sang the chorus the last time, knowing that their special summer together was ending. The chorus talked about how if friends have the Lord in their life, then they will be friends forever. The girls knew that would be the case for the four of them.

They were not looking forward to saying goodbye to each other, though.

Kendi saw the Brandons singing, as well as Amie's aunt and uncle. She heard later that the four of them had heard this song in person at a concert in Seattle when they were just teenagers.

Ryan, Ben, and some of the other high school kids were watching the girls sing.

Hope looked up and saw that Conner and his cousin Sarah were standing in the back seeing her sing…and cry, but she didn't even care. This was her moment…. hers and the other Guesthouse Girls.

Judy Ann Koglin

CHAPTER SEVENTEEN

Saying Goodbye

The next morning, the girls attended church with Aunty Nola. Amie's parents were there as well.

The sermon was about embracing change. The pastor used examples, such as caterpillars turning into butterflies and babies growing up and going on to do great things. He then talked about Abraham in Genesis and how he obeyed when God told him to leave and go elsewhere.

"Abraham embraced the change and did as God led," said the pastor. "Because of this, he became the father of the Jewish nation. In Hebrews, chapter 11, Abraham is included in a list of people who are commended for having great faith. Check it out if you aren't familiar with the chapter. Abraham was the father of Isaac, who was the father of Jacob, who was the father of the leaders of the 12 tribes.

179

What an honor! Abraham's obedience to God's call got this whole thing rolling. This is something huge, and Abraham would have missed out on it all if he didn't have the courage and the faith to leave his homeland and trust God.

"Now," the pastor continued, "if Abraham could trust God thousands of years ago to lead him to unknown parts where there could be all kinds of dangers and trials, do you think you might be able to trust Him with whatever it is that you are going through? Receiving salvation is a simple process, and many of you have already accepted that free gift. The Bible tells us that if we confess our sins, he will clean us up, forgive our sins, and we will live forever with Him. For a lot of us, that step of faith was easy. Think about it: who wouldn't want to accept the free gift of eternal life? For me, it was a no-brainer. So, most of us were able to muster up enough faith to trust God with our eternity. That's the hugest decision ever! But how about the smaller things? How many of us trust God to help us with the day-to-day stuff of life? With whom you should marry? With your career? With ethical decisions at work? With what house I should buy? Do you actually have faith that God has these things worked out for you, and His plan is way better than anything you could have imagined?

Don't we often forget that God cares about the smallest part of our lives. For you young people, the questions might be: Which college should I attend? Should I do track or tennis in the spring season? Who should I ask to the prom? Will I *ever* get a girlfriend?"

The congregation laughed at the exaggerated way he said that.

"Remember," the pastor said, "God is available 24/7, even for the small stuff. You can pray and ask Him to lead you. I promise He won't steer you wrong. Just have a little faith." With that, he led the congregation in a closing prayer, and everyone shuffled out into the lobby.

Amie's parents came up to their group.

Her dad was looking at a text on his phone and said, "Good news! The Olsens decided to check out early, so they are leaving tomorrow morning, and we can move back in as soon as the cleaner finishes.

"Awesome!" Amie grinned. She was looking forward to getting back to normal since school was starting up and she was eager to decorate her room. She saw Josh across the foyer, and they smiled and waved at each other.

"Doesn't he work at the resort?" her mother asked, seeing their interaction.

"Yes, in the restaurant," Amie replied nonchalantly. She wasn't ready to tell them that she was interested in him.

"Good-looking boy," her mom commented, and Amie gave a slight nod in agreement.

"Honey, we have some major catching up to do at the resort, so we probably won't see you until tomorrow morning," her dad announced to Amie.

"I'm actually going into work myself after lunch, so I might run into you there. Otherwise, I'll see you tomorrow!" Amie said enthusiastically. "It's nice to have you guys back!" Then, Amie decided this was possibly the best time to bring up the situation with driving. "So…do I get to start driving tomorrow?"

"We'll discuss it tomorrow," her dad replied with a smile. They exchanged hugs, and her parents left.

Amie rejoined Aunty Nola and the other girls who were cleaning up. Kendi and Hope cleared the last of the cups, and Emma folded the tablecloth that seemed to have avoided being spilled on. Amie folded up the white plastic table and carried it back to the storage closet and then they were ready to go.

Emma scurried on ahead to The Guesthouse, and the others took their last walk home from church together more leisurely.

When they approached the house, Kendi suggested that they walk around the back of the house to look at the ripening apples in the orchard.

As they walked out to the backyard together, they saw Emma standing behind the brand-new grill with Amie's big green taffeta bow on it.

"What is this?!" Aunty Nola asked, confused.

"It's from us, your Guesthouse Girls!" Emma cried, giving her a big hug.

"We wanted to get you something you needed," Amie added giving Aunty Nola a kiss on the cheek.

Kendi threw her arms around Aunty Nola. "We all pitched in!"

"We love you!" Hope added awkwardly, but sincerely.

Aunty Nola gathered the girls all together for a big group hug and had tears of joy in her eyes. "You all have been such a special group to have around this summer. You are like the daughters I never had. It's been a great summer with y'all."

Both Hope and Amie were going to have to leave right after lunch because their workplaces would be extra busy due to the holiday weekend crowds.

The girls had previously told Aunty Nola that they wanted to grill hamburgers for their last lunch together, so Aunty Nola had them thawed and seasoned in the fridge.

"I'd better get these burgers grilling," said Aunty Nola, "because I know you girls have places to be. I'm delighted to have this new grill to cook with!"

Aunty Nola got the grill going, and soon, they could smell the delightful aroma of the sizzling patties and the melting cheese.

The girls enjoyed their last lunch together for the summer. Amie and Hope were disappointed when they had to go to work, and they realized that this was their last chance to say goodbye to Kendi and Emma. Amie hugged first Emma then Kendi.

She had tears in her eyes when she told them how much she would miss them. "This was the best experience of my life, and you girls became my sisters from day one!"

The other girls tearfully agreed.

Hope was not usually emotional, but her eyes stung with unshed tears when she thought about their special little family splitting up and going their separate ways. She hugged Emma and Kendi and told them she would miss them and reminded them that they could do a ski weekend this winter.

Both Emma and Kendi told Hope how much they loved her and promised to stay in touch regularly.

"Keep us posted about the ski weekend!" Kendi told Hope. "I can imagine us four up on the slopes!"

After the goodbyes, Amie and Hope left for work.

****

Rachel Brandon had texted Kendi and Reed earlier and had asked them to stop by the coffee shop after lunch. The Brandons wanted to have a chance to say goodbye to the girls when there weren't customers around.

Rachel was putting up the closing sign when Kendi arrived. Reed was already there. Mark Brandon handed a thick envelope to each of the girls that included the tips from the week that was over double the size of a normal week. They also told the girls how thankful they were to have employed them this summer, and that both girls were invited to work for them again next summer.

"Reed, since you live close by, we might call you to see if you can cover vacations occasionally during the year, if you are interested."

Reed smiled. "Count me in!"

About that time, Reed's parents pulled up to pick her up and drive her back to her home in Manson. She hugged each of the others and thanked them for everything and went out to the car.

It was Kendi's turn next and she hugged Rachel and Mark Brandon. Then, Mrs. Brandon suggested that Ben walk her back to The Guesthouse. Kendi was surprised by that since it was broad daylight, but she agreed.

As Ben walked her home, he said how happy he was to get to know her this summer. He told her he originally wanted to date her from the first moment he saw her but thought it might be weird since they worked together.

"Then I decided, I don't care," Ben said, "I really like this girl...but then you told me that you weren't a Christian, so I decided that maybe we shouldn't get involved since we didn't see things the same."

"Was that when we were in your car that one time?" Kendi asked.

"Yes, I know I confused you, but I needed to end the flirtation, and I did it pretty suddenly," he explained. "I know that was rude, and I'm sorry."

"But then, I became a Christian..." Kendi said.

"Yes, but I didn't want to just pounce on you at that point. I felt like you needed time to figure out who you are in Christ, if that makes sense."

"I guess so," Kendi replied. "I'm still working on that."

"Then, we had so much fun puppy-sitting Duke together and then, the other day, I wanted to say something to you, but literally about the same time, Ryan walked in and asked you out. I know he has been interested in you all summer, so that was another complication."

"And then there was Emma," Kendi spoke slowly.

"And then there was Emma," Ben confirmed. "I think there was some attraction there as well, so the four of us were kind of in this crazy love square or whatever it was and none of us knew what to do, so we all did nothing, and that was probably for the best."

Kendi nodded.

"I know you are leaving in like an hour," Ben started. "I'm not asking for a commitment, but I was wondering if you might want to just continue our friendship through texting or maybe video chats sometimes. Nothing serious. I just want to keep connected, and maybe someday, the timing will work out for us. What do you think?"

"That sounds amazing!" Kendi agreed. They spent a few more minutes talking and then heard a car coming up the road. "My parents are here. I'd better go and get my bags."

"Okay, well, thanks for talking. I'm really glad I got to hang with you this summer. You are a special girl, Kendi," Ben said softly. He gave her a hug and walked away.

Kendi's dad parked the car, and her mom got out with a couple large shopping bags from Trader Joe's.

"I got Nola a few things," Mrs. Arnold admitted. "She doesn't have access to a lot of the cool stores here. Earlier this summer, she had told me some of her favorite things from Trader Joe's, and voila, here they are!"

"That is so sweet, Mom!" Kendi said. "Let's get my suitcases and say goodbye."

When she went into the house, Emma was sitting with Aunty Nola. Kendi went up, got her bags, and gave them to her dad, who took them out to the car.

Nola was thrilled with the items that Kendi's mom had brought her from Trader Joes, especially the cookies. The girls showed Kendi's parents the new barbecue grill that the girls had purchased from some of the money they earned this summer.

Kendi's parents were proud of the girls for their
initiative.

"I guess we'd better get on the road. Aunty Nola,
I can't thank you enough for all the love you gave
me this summer. You're wonderful!" Kendi said.

"Oh, Kendi," Aunty Nola murmured, stroking
her beautiful auburn hair, "I just love you, even
though I could never get you to our choir practice.
But hopefully, we'll see you on one of those
singing competitions on TV at some point."

"Not likely," Kendi laughed.

Turning to Emma, Kendi remarked, "And you,
little one," pulling her in a bear hug that lifted
Emma off her feet, "are my friend forever. I expect
lots of texts, and I will be the biggest fan of your
business blog when you publish it."

"I'll count on it. I'll need lots of interactions on
my posts to boost awareness," Emma laughed.
"Love you, friend!"

And with that, Kendi got into the car, closed the
door, and waved until she was out of sight.

Shortly after that, Emma's parents and her little
sister Riley pulled up. They had brought Aunty
Nola some nice grapes from their vineyard in
Pasco and a couple bottles of their signature white
wine. Nola joked about how this would liven up
her next committee meeting.

Another round of goodbyes was said then Emma left, leaving a piece of her heart behind in Chelan.

****

The next morning was Monday and Amie was up early and had packed all of her many bags including the extra suitcase she had her parents bring to fit the stuff from her summer shopping trips. She hugged Hope and Nola before her parents drove her home.

Amie told Hope that she would see her at school tomorrow and told Aunty Nola that she would see her at church. Both Amie and her parents thanked Aunty Nola profusely for allowing a local girl to stay in The Guesthouse this summer.

Aunty Nola explained, "Amie is not just any girl. She is special, and I wanted her here. She helped the other girls meet local friends and helped them learn more about the Lord. It was a pleasure to host her."

When everyone had left, Aunty Nola looked at Hope and said, "Ready to start your next chapter?"

Hope took a deep breath and let it out slowly, nodded and smiled, "Yes. I think I am."

Books in
The Guesthouse Girls Series

Summer Entanglements

Midsummer Adventures

Late Summer Love

Upcoming Books in
The Autumn Collection

The Autumn of Kendi

The Autumn of Hope

The Autumn of Emma

The Autumn of Amie

These books can be pre-ordered, as they are released, through Maui Shores Publishing. Sign up for our newsletter for release dates, giveaways, and sneak peeks of what's to come.

www.mauishorespublishing.com.

Acknowledgements

Much has happened in the seven months since I began writing these books and I have many people to thank. God has continued to amaze me by putting just the right people in my life to help me along the way. When I sop for a moment and break free from my own plans and my own agenda, I can take a moment and acknowledge the One who deserves all the praise, "In Him we live, and move, and have our being."

Living in a beautiful place, as many of us do, it is easy to fall into a trap of worshiping "created things" instead of "The Creator" as we are warned about in Scripture. So, with this tiny platform that I have been given, I want to acknowledge Him, and marvel at the miracles He can perform in all of us.

I also want to thank my faithful proofreaders: Kay and Kathy Koglin, and my mom, Nola Schulenburg, my wonderful editor, Savannah Cottrell @thewonderedits, my creative cover designer, Joanna Alonzo (www.joannaalonzo,com/services), my talented webmaster, Alex Stone, and my digital marketing coach, Liza Pierce @amauiblog. If you caught the online book launch, you saw my cousin's gorgeous Aloha Aku Inn. For rental info, check out www.alohaaku.com.

Last by not least, I want to thank Wade, my husband of over 28 years. We have a rare and wonderful marriage built on enduring friendship, storybook love, and mutual respect. Wade you are truly my better half and your encouragement allows me to follow my heart into all kinds of adventures.

Note from the Author

As I am writing this, we just finished the book launch <u>Summer Entanglements</u> and <u>Midsummer Adventures,</u> book one and two in The Guesthouse Girls series, and this book is about to be published. We hope that you have enjoyed the summer at The Guesthouse with Amie, Emma, Hope, and Kendi.

Fortunately, we have four more books about The Guesthouse Girls ready to go through the channels to be published and I'll get started writing the next ones soon. The next four books will be called The Autumn Collection. Each book will center on one of the girls in the fall semester of her junior year, set in her own hometown and school. Don't worry, although the girls will be split up, there will be plenty of interaction between the "core four" in each book so you won't have to wait to get updates on your favorite Guesthouse Girl!

If you read these books, I'd love to hear your comments and questions. Please engage with me on social media:
Facebook: The Guesthouse Girls (@theguesthousegirlsbooks)
Instagram: @judyannkoglin_author and @mauishorespublishing
Sign up for my newsletter to get updates, freebies, and tips at <u>www.mauishorespublishing.com</u>

About the Author

Judy Ann Koglin grew up in the Seattle area, then attended Washington State University in Pullman.

In her teens and twenties, Judy Ann enjoyed several trips to Chelan and found it to be a magical town. She also spent a teenage summer working in a charming beachside area on the Puget Sound, and she draws on both of these experiences to weave coming-of-age stories such as the ones in The Guesthouse Girls series.

In 2017 Judy Ann and Wade fulfilled a long-time dream and moved to the island of Maui. Together, they are the proud parents of two boys, Tyler and Tim, and a daughter in-law Lauren.

Printed in Great Britain
by Amazon